A Forever Kind of Love

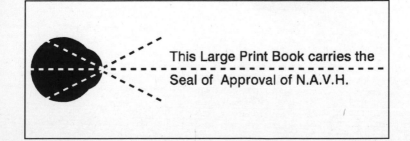

This Large Print Book carries the
Seal of Approval of N.A.V.H.

BAYOU DREAMS

A Forever Kind
of Love

Farrah Rochon

THORNDIKE PRESS
A part of Gale, Cengage Learning

GALE
CENGAGE Learning·

Farmington Hills, Mich • San Francisco • New York • Waterville, Maine
Meriden, Conn • Mason, Ohio • Chicago

LIBRARY OF CONGRESS CATALOGING-IN-PUBLICATION DATA

Rochon, Farrah.
  A forever kind of love / by Farrah Rochon. — Large print edition.
    pages ; cm. — (Bayou dreams ; #1) (Thorndike Press large print African-American)
    ISBN 978-1-4104-7434-6 (hardcover) — ISBN 1-4104-7434-8 (hardcover)
    1. African Americans—Fiction. 2. Large type books. I. Title.
PS3618.O346F667 2014
813'.6—dc23   2014031496

Published in 2014 by arrangement with Harlequin Books S.A.

Printed in Mexico
1 2 3 4 5 6 7 18 17 16 15 14

Dear Reader,

When I was a little girl I was fascinated by the big city, with its bright lights and tall buildings. It wasn't until years later that I came to appreciate the true charm of small-town life. The mom-and-pop stores, friendly faces and yes, even the gossip — they all combine to create a sense of community that warms my heart.

That's what I've tried to depict with the fictional town of Gauthier. I drew upon my own experiences growing up in a tiny town on the Louisiana bayou to show how supportive close-knit communities can be. May you feel as at home in Gauthier as I do.

I hope you enjoy this first book in my Bayou Dreams series.

Be sure to look me up online at Facebook, Twitter and my website, www.farrahrochon .com.

Blessing,
Farrah Rochon

Dedicated to the residents of
my small hometown.

The community of believers was one in
heart and mind. No one claimed that any
of their possessions was their own, but
they shared everything they had.

— *Acts* 4:32

Many thanks to Pat Duncan at the Louisiana Office of Cultural Development: Division of Historic Preservation for generously providing her expertise. Any mistakes regarding historic building preservation and the National Register are my own.

CHAPTER 1

The tips of black four-inch heels sank into the soft earth, blades of grass fanning around the base of the slim pedestals. The shoes were the first things he noticed about her, but now his eyes traveled upward, taking in the thin, gold ankle bracelet underneath stockings so sheer they were almost invisible.

Her black skirt was shorter than most in this small town deemed decent for such an occasion. It hugged her hips and cupped her perfect rear end. His eyes continued their slow trek, passed her delicately rounded shoulders, to her unyielding neck and finally to the wide-brimmed black hat tilted at an angle atop her proud head.

Mya Dubois stood before the charcoal-gray casket holding a single-stemmed white rose he'd seen her slip from the generous spray draping the head end of the casket. She'd stood in that same position for the

11

past ten minutes, preventing the cemetery workers from lowering the coffin into the ground. He'd caught several shared looks of agitation between the workers, but they seemed resigned to it. They must be used to guilt-laden family members holding up their day.

Corey Anderson pushed away from the wall of the stone mausoleum he'd been resting against and walked over to where she stood, stopping a foot behind her.

"Welcome back home, Peaches."

Her back became even straighter, that proud neck stiffening even more.

"And here I was hoping to get through the day without speaking to you," Mya said without turning around, her bland words laced with sarcasm.

"And here I was hoping you'd left that sass back in New York City," Corey replied, unable to keep the tinge of amusement from his voice. Not really appropriate given where they were standing. "Come on, Peaches. These guys need to finish their work."

"Can I finish saying goodbye to my grandfather?" she snapped.

Corey looked over at the two workers. One held up his gloved hands in a "what can you do?" gesture. He heard a delicate sniff, and

Corey's heart softened just a bit as he saw Mya's shaking hand wipe at the trail of tears that had begun cascading down her cheek.

She looked over at the two cemetery workers. "Thank you for waiting." Then she did an about-face and headed in the direction of the church hall.

Corey was next to her in three strides. "Mind if I attempt to be a gentleman and escort you?"

"I can manage," she answered.

"Peaches, don't be this way."

She stopped and turned. She sauntered up to him, one delicate brow raised over her topaz-colored eyes. "That's the last time I hear you say the word *peaches*," she said with quiet warning. "Even if you're eating one, you'd better call it a plum. You hear me?"

This time Corey didn't try to stop the smile from pulling at the corner of his mouth. Very few people in the small town of Gauthier, Louisiana, could talk to him in that tone of voice and get away with it.

And only one could look so good while doing it.

Damn, he'd missed her. As far as he knew, this was Mya's first trip back to Gauthier since she'd left over fifteen years ago, and Corey doubted she would stay one minute longer than necessary. She probably had her boarding pass tucked inside that little black purse she'd been clutching throughout her grandfather's funeral service.

Mya took off again for the church hall. Corey followed a few steps behind, admiring the view. How she managed to balance on those sexy heels once they reached the gravel parking lot was beyond his comprehension, but that was the case with just about everything Mya Dubois had ever done in her life. Why should this be any different?

Mya pushed off with her toe, setting the porch swing on a gentle sway. Her iced tea had grown watery, but she sipped anyway, hoping to quell the heat.

"Springtime in Louisiana," Mya murmured as she used her forehead to wipe condensation from the glass. She could go back into the air-conditioned house, but the atmosphere in there was more oppressing than these record-high temperatures.

Mya knew she should have booked her flight for this afternoon. Guilt had forced her to add another day to her trip, but with Elizabeth milking the grieving-daughter role for all it was worth and the houseful of nosy neighbors prying into her life, Mya wanted nothing more than to be on a flight back to New York.

Maybe she could come back in a few weeks. Then she could sit back and enjoy a rare visit back home with her grandparents.

Her grandmother. Granddad was no longer here.

Mya took another sip of tea. It had a hard time flowing past the lump in her throat. Maybe she *should* go back in the house. She'd rather be curled up in Granddad's old recliner, inhaling the scent of his pipe smoke. But the thought of facing the dozens of townsfolk who'd followed them back to the house after the repast at the church hall kept her butt planted firmly on the swing.

If she had to hear one more *I'm so sorry for your loss,* she would start screaming and never stop, which was why she'd changed into a pair of khaki capris and a sleeveless V-neck tee and had escaped to the porch nearly an hour ago. Mya welcomed the solitude like the unexpected breeze that blew every so often. She knew she should be social and help entertain the well-wishers who'd come to help her family grieve, but her grandma, Aunt Maureen and her mother, Elizabeth, were in there, and if there was one thing Elizabeth Dubois knew how to do, it was work a crowd.

Mya heard the squeak of the screen door's hinges, followed moments later by, "What are you doing out here?"

Speak of the devil. Still wearing her Prada pumps, no doubt.

"I'm enjoying this nice spring day," Mya answered with a drawl as her mother walked over to the swing.

"Nice?" Elizabeth scoffed. "It feels as if it's a hundred degrees out here. Al Gore warned everyone about global warming."

Mya rolled her eyes, placing her glass of iced tea on the thick railing that ran across the top of the porch.

Her mother waited for the swing to sway forward then sat on the opposite end from Mya. "So, how's it been, honey?" She patted Mya's knee as if it were the most natural thing in the world for the two of them to chitchat like a normal mother and daughter. *Normal* and *Elizabeth Dubois* should never be used in the same sentence.

"Let's not do this," Mya implored.

"I'm just trying to make conversation," her mother said in that prim and proper way that went down Mya's spine like fingernails on a chalkboard.

"When you have to *try,* that's a good indication that two people probably shouldn't be conversing."

Elizabeth's perfectly made-up face twisted with reproach. "When did you become so angry?"

Mya squinted as if thinking hard. "Around 2007 or so. March, if I remember correctly. Snagged my favorite panty hose on the subway. Everything's just gone downhill since then."

Her mother stood. "I don't know why I even try to talk to you."

"Makes two of us," Mya murmured underneath her breath. She watched her mother walk back through the door she'd just come from, her entire body heaving a sigh of relief.

Even if she were up for drama today, she still wouldn't give Elizabeth the satisfaction. A post-funeral catfight would be the hand her mother fanned. She would play the victim card until its edges were tattered.

Mya pushed the swing again, then brought her other leg up and wrapped her arms around them, resting her head on her knees.

She wasn't an angry person; Elizabeth just brought out the worst in her. Always had. Mya knew it wasn't healthy to hold such a long-standing grudge, but despite many attempts, she just could not let go of the resentment she felt toward her mother.

Maybe if she had ever, just once, sensed

17

an ounce of regret in Elizabeth for walking away from her own child.

"Yeah, right," Mya snorted.

The few times Elizabeth had bothered to visit after leaving Mya's grandparents to raise her, she spent the entire time talking about the glamorous life she was leading with whomever happened to be her boyfriend at the time. She'd tell Mya she needed to straighten her hair, learn to flirt, do whatever it took to attract a man so he could rescue her away from this godforsaken town, before she ended up like her Aunt Maureen. Mya would prefer to be like Maureen over Elizabeth any day of the week and twice on Sunday.

Mya had made it out of Gauthier, but she'd done it on her own. She hadn't needed anyone to *rescue* her. And, unlike Elizabeth, she hadn't left a baby for others to raise.

Even though she'd come close.

Mya shook off the disturbing thought. She continued to sway, pulling in deep breaths as the swing rocked back, letting them out when she went forward. She'd love to spend the rest of the afternoon out here, but it was time to go into the house and face the judgmental stares. Every expression said the same thing: it took her grandfather dying to

18

bring Mya Dubois back to Gauthier.

Just as she reached out to grab the rail post, the swing stopped and Corey Anderson plopped down next to her. She hadn't even heard him approach.

She had managed to avoid him since their meet and greet in the cemetery. It was a trend Mya wanted to continue.

"Believe it or not, I was just leaving," she said, rising from the swing.

"You don't want to go in there," he warned her.

She glanced at him and raised her brows in question.

"Act two," Corey answered. "A solo performance by the great Elizabeth Dubois. Someone picked up one of your granddad's pipes, and she went into hysterics. Last I saw, three people were holding her up and one was fanning her."

Mya clenched her fists at her sides and opened her mouth in a silent scream toward the sky. She resumed her seat on the swing, bringing one leg up again and resting her chin against her knee.

"You think I could get away with shaking her senseless just one time, or would I go to jail for assault?" she asked.

Corey shrugged as he looked out over the yard. "Kandice Lewis is the district attorney now. Doesn't she still owe you a favor for filling in on the cheerleading squad when she was too drunk to make the games?"

"Stop it." Mya laughed. "She suffered from some kind of stomach thing. I doubt Kandice has ever been drunk a day in her life."

"She was always one of the good girls."

"Unlike me?"

"You said it," Corey returned with a chuckle. Mya caught him with an elbow to the arm. "Hey." He held up his hands. "I always liked the bad girls."

"Only fair, since you're the one who helped them earn their reputations in the first place."

Mya watched his profile as a slow smile drew across his face. She could only imagine what was going through that pretty little head of his.

She couldn't deny that he was still pretty, though Corey would throttle her for using that particular word to describe him. Mr. Macho Baseball Hero never considered himself *pretty*, but with that strong jaw and those signature light brown Anderson eyes, Corey was not just pretty, he was as gorgeous as ever.

Mya was touched that he'd returned for her granddad's funeral. Coming back to

Gauthier was probably as hard for Corey as it had been for her. As far as Mya knew, he no longer had family here. According to her grandmother, the last of the Andersons, his eldest brother, Leon, had moved somewhere up north after their father died of a heart attack a few years ago. It was the same thing that had taken their mother during Corey's first year of high school. The two middle boys, the twins, Stefan and Shawn, had both left with the assistance of the legal system.

Baseball had saved Corey from a similar fate, but for most of his youth, he had been as bad as his twin brothers. Especially when it came to her. With her he had been deliciously bad. The kind of bad that made a girl's toes curl and her skin tingle. God, it had been a long time since she'd had that kind of bad in her life.

If only things had ended differently.

Mya put a choke hold on those thoughts and wrestled them back to the corner of her mind she wasn't allowed to visit unless she was drowning her sorrows in a glass of merlot. Today had been enough of an emotional brain suck; she didn't need the ghosts of her past mistakes adding to her inevitable breakdown.

"Gosh, I'm just ready for this day to be over." Mya pushed her fingers through the

21

tight, springy ringlets that her naturally curly hair produced when dried by the sun.

"Been rough on you, huh?" Corey asked.

She hunched her shoulders. "I just thought he would be here longer, you know? He always used to say that dying wasn't an option."

"Sounds like something Big Harold would say." Corey chuckled. He pushed the swing with his foot, then stretched his right arm across the back.

Mya let the motion lull her back to that calm place she'd found before her mother had interrupted her peace. Her bare foot lightly grazed the porch's floorboards as it swayed back and forth. The paint had started to peel in spots, another indicator that Granddad had been suffering with cancer long before he let anyone know. There's no way he would have allowed any part of this house to go downhill if he'd been feeling well enough to fix it.

If she had been here, maybe she would have seen the pain in his eyes.

Guilt twisted in her gut, but Mya accepted the pain as penance. She looked out over the yard of the house where she'd spent the first seventeen years of her life. Cars were parked haphazardly within the fenced-in portion, while others lined both sides of the street. Everyone had respected the side yard where Granddad's vegetable garden brimmed with plump tomatoes drooping from the vine, flowering heads of cabbage, peppers, okra and about a dozen other vegetables that had fed the people in this small town for years.

Before she returned to New York she would pick the vegetables that were ready. She couldn't stand the thought of the fruits of Granddad's hard work falling to the ground and dying.

Mya blew out a shaky breath, willing the tears to remain at bay.

"It was a nice service," Corey said after a stretch of surprisingly comfortable silence. Though it wasn't all that surprising. She and Corey had always been at ease with each other. That had been part of her downfall.

"Granddad deserved it," Mya said. "He's probably walking around heaven with his chest sticking out, bragging about all the people who showed up for his funeral."

"People around here loved Big Harold."

Mya simply nodded. If she tried to speak, the tears would start flowing again.

Too late.

She swiped at the moisture that had collected in the corner of her eye. "Don't even try it," she said when she saw Corey's hand reach for her. "Just because we're talking, it doesn't mean you can touch me. Keep those paws right where they are."

He held his hands up, then placed them on his thighs. Mya studied the fingers fanned out across his black slacks. The nails were clean, cut nice and short. He'd always taken extra care in making sure he didn't bear the telltale signs of an auto mechanic like his dad.

All those years ago, when they would lay wrapped in each other's arms talking about their futures, Corey used to tell her that he refused to get trapped in the family tradition of fixing cars for a living. It's what his twin brothers had done in between their many run-ins with the law.

After an incident that nearly landed him in jail, Corey had turned his life around in their senior year of high school. He did everything he could to show the people in Gauthier that he was not going to follow in Shawn and Stefan's footsteps. Yet the people around here had lumped him in with his brothers anyway.

"Thanks for coming back here for Granddad's funeral," Mya felt the need to say. Facing the judgmental tongues of Gauthier could not have been easy for him.

He stared at her for a long, drawn-out moment before finally answering with a simple, "You're welcome."

She zoomed in on the curve of his jaw. His skin was still smooth, that beautiful, roasted pecan color. It was marred by a thin strip of pink that stretched from his ear almost to his neck.

"What happened here?" Mya asked, trailing her finger along the slightly puckered skin. Touching him was a mistake. Her finger burned hot.

He turned to her, those light, grayish-brown eyes taking on that smoldering look that was the precursor to her panties sliding off back in high school.

"Car accident," Corey answered. "About three years ago."

His voice had lowered. It had the same effect as his gaze. Both caused her heart to beat faster within the walls of her chest.

No way. She was not going there again with Corey Anderson.

Mya tore her eyes away and sat up straight. "I need to get inside."

"I'll come with you," Corey said, pushing himself up from the swing.

"No." She put a hand on his shoulder, then jerked it back. *Stop touching him!* "I don't need you to follow me."

"Peach— Mya," he corrected. "I'm trying to be a nice guy. It's been fifteen years. All that stuff should be behind us."

That's what scared her. It *should* be behind her. But one look at those sexy eyes and that just-right-for-her mouth and she was that stupid teenage girl who used to escape out the window of this very house to be with him.

"It is behind us," Mya lied. "I'm just tired. It's been a rough day. I'm going to go inside, kiss a few cheeks, say a few good-byes and head to one of the back rooms for a nap."

"You sure?"

She nodded. With a slight smile, she said, "It was good seeing you, Corey." And she meant it. It *was* good to see him. Despite the agony Corey Anderson had unwittingly put her through, a part of her heart would always belong to him.

And if that wasn't reason enough to get her butt back to New York, Mya didn't know what was.

"Thanks again for coming to the funeral," she said.

Against her better judgment, Mya leaned over and placed a kiss on his cheek. Then she quickly headed into the house, escaping temptation.

26

■ ■ ■ ■

Corey watched Mya slip back into her grandparents' house and had to force himself not to follow her. His skin tingled where her lips had touched, warming his body from the inside out.

How could she still have this effect on him?

His heart had started beating triple time when she'd walked through the doors of New Hope Baptist Church that morning. The small sanctuary seemed to have shrunk around him. Throughout the entire service, the only thing Corey could focus on was the woman who'd been a girl the last time he'd laid eyes on her.

There had been speculation over whether or not Mya would return to Gauthier for her grandfather's funeral. Corey could not deny the bone-deep relief he'd felt the minute he set eyes on her in the church. He'd smiled at her — a smile she had not returned — and Corey figured that maybe fifteen years had not been enough time for Mya to get over what had happened the night of their high school graduation.

Not that he could blame her.

Regret lanced his chest as the image of

her pained face jumped to the forefront of his mind. He would never forget the moment he'd looked up and found her staring at him through the window of his dad's truck, where he'd sat half-naked with another girl's legs wrapped around his waist. It was in that moment — when he knew he'd lost her — that Corey had realized just how lucky he had been to have her in the first place.

He had been a selfish, inconsiderate fool who deserved every dirty look Mya threw his way, even fifteen years later.

Corey had considered keeping his distance after the funeral. With half the town in attendance, it would have been easy to convince himself that there wasn't an opportunity for any one-on-one time with her. But when had he ever chosen to take the easy path where Mya was concerned?

After that kiss, as innocent as it had been, Corey was happy he'd decided to seek her out. He rubbed his cheek, still experiencing the lingering effects of her soft lips on his skin. Despite how things had ended between them all those years ago, Mya Dubois could still affect him like no other woman could.

CHAPTER 2

A thick slice of sun slashed across the bed, warming her face and forcing one eye to open.

"Curtains, Gram. Curtains that close would be a nice touch," Mya murmured into the pillow. She rolled onto her back and stared at the ceiling. Someone had tried to paint over the brown water stain left from when the air-conditioning ducts had backed up, but Mya could still make out the faint edges. The stain had always reminded her of a bunny rabbit playing in the grass.

Mya reached for her eyeglasses from the nightstand. After sliding her feet into a pair of flip-flops, she didn't bother to throw a robe on over her boy shorts and tank top. Now that Granddad was gone, there were only women in the house.

The aroma of sweet chicory coffee greeted her as she stepped into the hallway, along with the voices of her grandmother, Aunt

Mo and her mother. Of course, Elizabeth was the loudest. Mya rushed through her morning bathroom routine and then headed straight for the liquid caffeine.

"Good morning," she said as she entered the kitchen.

Aunt Mo was at the stove, stirring a pot of what looked like grits. Grandma and Elizabeth sat at the table. Her mother was dressed to the nines. Mya spotted a Christian Dior suitcase and a round hatbox just to the right of the door, and she nearly whooped with glee. She was more than ready to see Elizabeth board a plane back to San Francisco or Seattle or wherever it was she was living these days. Mya had stopped keeping track.

"You want breakfast?" Aunt Mo asked.

"No, thanks. The coffee's enough for me."

"You need more than just coffee," her grandmother chastised.

"It's better if she skips breakfast," Elizabeth chimed in. "You don't want to get fat. Right, baby?"

Deep breaths, Mya told herself. *In through the nose, out through the mouth.*

She grabbed a mug from the wooden mug tree and filled the cup almost to the brim. "Any sweetener?" she asked her aunt.

"I ran out of artificial sweetener last

week," Grandma said.

"Have you been eating sugar again?" Aunt Mo asked.

"Don't start with me, Maureen."

Her aunt plunked her free hand on her hip as the other continued to stir the grits. "That woman is too hardheaded for me."

Mya winked at her grandmother as she walked past the table on her way to the smaller porch just off the kitchen. The morning was too pretty to take her coffee anywhere but outside. She sat on the wooden porch step and sipped her coffee, closing her eyes in pure ecstasy as the hot liquid slid down her throat.

"Thank God for coffee." She sighed.

A motorized roar jolted Mya out of her relaxed, caffeine-induced bliss. She looked up to find Corey dressed in knee-length deck shorts — the kind with a dozen zippered pockets all over them — and a green T-shirt. He was pushing a lawn mower across the side lawn. He lifted his hand in a short wave, turned a tight corner with the lawn mower and headed back up toward the front yard.

"What the hell?" Mya muttered. She placed her coffee cup on the step and stomped across the yard.

"Corey!" she yelled.

31

He ignored her.

No, he hadn't ignored her. Mya spotted the thin, white wires coming from his ears. She caught up to him and tapped him on the shoulder. The lawn mower sputtered to a stop as Corey let go of the handle. He turned, pulling the tiny speakers from his ears.

"Good morning," he said.

"What are you doing here?"

"That question rhetorical?" he asked, motioning to the lawn mower. "What are *you* doing here? I thought you'd be on a plane by now."

"I fly out this afternoon," Mya answered. "Now answer my question. What are you doing here?"

He shrugged. "It's Saturday. I always cut your grandmother's grass every other Saturday."

Wait. *What?*

He folded his arms over his green Gauthier High School Fighting Lions T-shirt and things started to click into place.

"You live here?" she asked. "In Gauthier?"

He nodded, a smile crinkling the corners of his eyes. Those eyes drifted a few degrees south and his smile widened. That's when Mya remembered she was standing in the middle of the yard in boy shorts, a thin tank top and no bra. She crossed her arms over her breasts.

"When did you move back to Gauthier?" she asked.

Another shrug. "Last year."

"Why?" She couldn't keep the incredulousness from her voice. He'd retired from professional baseball a few years ago, but Mya knew Corey was still worth millions. Why would he choose to live in a small town like Gauthier when he could live anywhere he wanted to?

"It's home," he answered.

Before she could respond, a screech from inside the house stopped her.

"Mya!"

The panic in Aunt Mo's scream caused instant fear to race down Mya's spine. Corey had already taken off in a dead run for the house. She shook off her shock and followed, losing a flip-flop along the way.

Mya's stomach bottomed out at the sight in the kitchen.

Her grandmother was slumped over in the chair, her mouth hanging open. Aunt Maureen had hooked her arms under Grandma's, trying to lift her up. Corey was crouched on the floor in front of her, tapping on her cheek. Elizabeth was off to the side, wringing her hands and screaming uncontrollably.

"Would you shut up!" Mya yelled at her mother. She held her grandmother's wrist to check for a pulse, enjoying a moment's relief after finding one.

"She has these fainting spells, but never like this," Aunt Mo said.

Mya leaned in. "Grandma, can you hear me?" The sickly sweet smell hovering in front of her grandmother's face was all the answer Mya needed. "I don't think this is a fainting spell. Mama, call 911."

"What? Why?" Elizabeth cried.

Mya ran over to where her mother stood and pushed her aside so she could get to the phone mounted on the wall.

"I have a seventy-two-year-old female with diabetes," she told the 911 operator. "She passed out and isn't responding and her breath has a fruity smell."

Mya rattled off the address. She hung up and ran back to the table, prying her Aunt Maureen from her grandmother. "Aunt Mo, get all of her medications. We'll need to bring them to the hospital." Mya took her place, slipping her arms underneath her grandmother's armpits and holding her upright. She looked down at Corey who was still trying to get her to wake up.

He looked up at her and shook his head.

Mya's chest tightened.

"She'll need her insulin," Corey said. "Miss Elizabeth, look in the fridge. She keeps the insulin in a Tupperware container."

How does he know that? The whirl of the ambulance sirens stopped Mya from voicing the question out loud.

Moments later, two uniformed EMS workers entered the kitchen carrying a gurney. Mya stood to the side, fear gripping her chest as they checked her grandmother's vitals, then strapped her to the gurney. She felt warm, gritty arms surround her as Corey came up behind her, encircling her in his arms.

Mya could hardly comprehend the scene unfolding before her eyes. This could not be happening. She'd just buried her granddad yesterday. She was *not* staring at her grandmother on a hospital gurney.

But she was. This was real.

Mya snapped out of her trance and shook out of Corey's embrace. "Aunt Mo, you ride in the ambulance. I'll follow behind."

They followed the gurney outside. Mya watched as they loaded her grandmother into the back of the ambulance, then she ran to her bedroom and stripped out of her shorts, pulling on a pair of jeans and a roomy T-shirt over her tank top. She was back in the kitchen in less than two minutes.

Corey was drying his hands on a dish towel. "You ready?" he asked.

"Uh, yes. Where's Elizabeth?" she asked.

"She took Maureen's car to the hospital. I told her I'd drive you."

"Okay," Mya said with a shaky breath. She looked around the kitchen, unsure of what she was searching for. Maybe there was something they would need at the hospital. Mya didn't realize she was trembling until Corey caught her upper arms.

"She's going to be okay," he said.

She stared into his confident eyes. It was easy to believe words said with such conviction. Mya fed off of it.

"Yes, she will," she answered.

Corey gave her shoulders a light squeeze. "Then let's get out of here. Your grandmother needs you."

She nodded, for once grateful for his presence. "Let's go."

In the twenty minutes it had taken them to reach the small hospital in Maplesville, right outside of Gauthier, Mya had managed to work herself into another fit of nerves. They weighed heavy in her stomach, twisting and tangling like snakes in a hot skillet.

What if something happened to her grandmother?

"No," Mya said out loud.

"What?" Corey asked from the driver's
seat. He'd driven fifteen miles over the
posted speed limit from the moment they'd
pulled away from the house, maneuvering
his bulky Cadillac Escalade as if it were a
sleek sports car. "Mya." He waited for her
to look at him. "She's going to be okay."

"You don't know that," Mya said with a
catch in her voice.

"Your grandmother is even more stubborn
than Big Harold was. She's not going
anywhere for a long time."

They pulled up to the hospital's emergency room entrance, and Mya was out of
the SUV before it came to a complete stop.

"Sir, you have to move your vehicle. This
is a restricted area," she heard someone tell
Corey.

She ran to the nurses' station. "Eloise
Dubois?" she asked. "She was brought in
after fainting."

"Mya!" Maureen called.

Mya raced toward her aunt. "How is she?"

"I don't know yet, but she was awake by
the time we got here."

"Thank God," Mya cried.

"Come on." Her aunt took her elbow.

"The nurse said she'd come find us in the waiting room."

Mya followed, anxiety still shooting through her veins. She crumpled into the closest chair, not trusting her legs to hold her up a second longer. She cradled her face in her hands and took a couple of slow, deep breaths. Aunt Mo sat in the chair next to her and rubbed her hand up and down Mya's arm.

"How'd this happen, Aunt Mo?"

"Because she's hardheaded and doesn't like to take care of herself." Maureen shook her head. "I know part of it is my fault. With everything going on this week with Daddy's funeral, I haven't been paying as much attention as I should. I usually make sure she checks her blood sugar."

"Don't start blaming yourself."

"Oh, I'm not blaming myself entirely. She's a grown woman, and she knows what she should and shouldn't do. But like I said, she's hardheaded. People have been bringing food over to the house around the clock, and she's been nibbling on everything. I know they mean well, but it just makes it harder to keep the wrong foods out of Mama's mouth."

Familiar guilt assailed Mya once again. It wasn't solely up to Aunt Maureen to take care of Grandma. Mya should have been here helping. Her grandparents had raised her since the age of three, after her mother had decided to leave Gauthier and make a life for herself with the first in a string of men.

It was the best thing that could have happened to Mya. Her grandparents had always been there for her, but she had not done the same in return.

Corey stalked into the waiting room. "How is she?" he asked.

"We're still waiting on the nurse," Aunt Mo answered.

He sat in the seat across from Mya, his knees braced apart. Snippets of grass clung to the short hairs on his legs.

"You don't have to stay," Mya told him.

"I'm not leaving until I know Mrs. Eloise is okay," he answered.

"I can call —"

"Don't try to explain anything to him," Aunt Mo said. "He's as stubborn as your grandmother, which is why they get along so well."

"You and my grandmother get along?" Mya blurted. "She hated you when we were growing up."

"She got over it," Corey said in a clipped voice that clearly told Mya to do the same.

He rested his elbows on his thighs and clasped his hands together.

The aroma of sweat, grass and dirt hit Mya square in the face, reminding her of how he'd smelled when he would come to her after baseball practice, not bothering to take a shower. In her horny, sex-crazed teenage mind, it hadn't mattered one bit. They would go at it like rabbits in the cab of his daddy's dusty pickup, parked under that big pecan tree in old Mr. Herbert's field.

Mya tore her eyes away from his toned brown legs. She didn't need any reminders of those long-ago mistakes.

Corey rose. "I need coffee," he said. "Anybody else want some?"

"I'd love some," Maureen answered. "There isn't any here, though. The nurse said the coffeemaker is broken."

"There's a little place right next door called Drusilla's. They sell good egg-and-cheese sandwiches. You want something to eat?"

"Just the coffee," Aunt Mo answered.

"Mya?" Corey asked.

She shook her head. "I'm fine." Truth was Mya didn't trust her stomach to keep anything down. She was a ball of nerves. She doubted the condition would improve until she saw her grandmother alert and well.

Minutes passed with only the low hum of a late-model television mounted in the corner making any noise. It was the quiet peacefulness that alerted Mya that something was missing. "Where's Elizabeth?" she asked Aunt Mo.

"I don't know," her aunt said with an agitated wave of her hand. "The gift shop, I think."

"She would find somewhere to shop," Mya snorted.

"That's how she calms herself down. Don't complain. I'd rather her out there bothering those people than in here bothering me."

"I know you had the chance to drown her at birth," Mya said.

Aunt Mo nodded. "I should have taken it. Though you wouldn't be here."

"It's a sacrifice I'd have made to save the planet from Elizabeth Dubois."

As if she'd heard her name, her mother burst through the waiting room door, followed by a doctor in green scrubs and white tennis shoes.

"She's going to be okay," Elizabeth cried.

Mya jumped from her seat and rushed over to the doctor, trying not to hold her high blond ponytail and Hello Kitty earrings against her. Mya wasn't too keen on her grandmother's life resting in the hands of someone who looked barely out of medical school.

"How is she?" Mya asked. "Can we see her?"

"She's going to be fine," the doctor answered patiently. "You'll be able to see her soon."

"What happened?" Mya asked.

"Well, her blood glucose levels were extremely high —"

"But she's okay now?" Maureen cut the doctor off.

The doctor nodded.

"Thank you, God." Mya collapsed into the chair nearest the door. Elizabeth was the one who usually favored dramatics, but relief that she would not bury both grandparents within a week was so overwhelming, it knocked Mya's legs right from under her.

"Can we bring her home today?" Aunt Mo asked.

The doctor's eyes darted around the room. "Can you all follow me?" she asked.

Anxiety thrummed through Mya's veins at the seriousness she sensed in the doctor's voice. "What's wrong? Is she really okay?"

"Yes. Yes. I'm sorry. I didn't mean to alarm you. There are a couple of things we need to discuss regarding Mrs. Dubois's care, and patient confidentiality prevents us from discussing it here in the waiting room."

Mya accepted the explanation with a nod, but still walked on shaky legs as they followed the doctor to a room two doors down. The square plaque next to the door had *Privacy Room* embossed on it in raised letters.

"Is my mother going to die?" Elizabeth asked as soon as the door closed.

"Not anytime soon," the doctor answered. "*If* she continues to take her insulin and monitor her blood sugar levels. However, we did see an abnormality on her initial blood scan. We want to keep her to run a few more tests."

"What type of abnormality?" Maureen asked.

"I don't know enough yet. Any time flags are raised on the blood tests of a diabetic, we take it seriously. I'd rather be overly cautious than miss something and see her back here in a few weeks."

"Do whatever you need to do," Mya said. "As long as she's okay."

"Absolutely," the doctor answered with a smile. "I'll send a nurse to the waiting room

43

to let you all know when you can see her."

The morning had been an emotional roller coaster, but at least they now had the doctor's word that her grandmother would be okay. Mya welcomed the muscle-relaxing flood of relief that rushed through her body.

"Well, I guess I should call myself a cab. It's time for me to get out of here," Elizabeth announced.

The muscles in Mya's neck and shoulders instantly tensed. "What do you mean it's time for you to get out of here?"

"My plane leaves in three hours. I'm running late as it is. It'll take me at least an hour to get to the airport, and I wanted to stop in New Orleans for a few things before I fly out."

"Mother, are you seriously leaving while your mother is in the hospital? Before even going in to see her?"

"Don't be so dramatic, Mya. I swear you should be on the theater stage instead of designing costumes for other actors."

Mya turned to her aunt, who stood at the door to the privacy room, her hands crossed over her chest. "Did *she* just call *me* dramatic?" Mya asked.

"Just let it go, Mya. Let *her* go."

"Yes, please, let me go," Elizabeth said. "It's time for me to get back to civilization.

I swear I don't know how you people in Gauthier can stand it. There's not even a Starbucks."

Anger simmered beneath Mya's skin. She had been just as anxious to get back to New York, but there was no way she could leave with her grandmother in the hospital. Apparently, Elizabeth didn't share the same sense of responsibility.

"You will never change," Mya huffed with a disgusted snort. "I don't know why I expected anything different from you."

"Well, I certainly won't stand here while you look down your nose at me." Elizabeth stalked over to the door in her high-heeled sandals. "Tell Mama I'll see her next time I'm in town. And take better care of her, Maureen."

"You have the nerve —" Mya started, but her aunt raised her hand, cutting her off.

"I will take better care of her. Now go on. You've got a plane to catch."

Elizabeth nodded and, without another word, turned and walked out of the privacy room.

As soon as she was gone, Mya stomped up to her aunt. "Why would you let her talk to you that way? As if it's your fault that Grandma is in the hospital."

"Haven't you learned that the best way to

deal with your mother is to say whatever is necessary to get her gone?"

"But Grandma is just as much her responsibility as she is yours," Mya pointed out. "I hate how she treats you, Aunt Mo. And the way she walks around as if she's better than everybody? It just sickens me."

"Mya, your mother has been that way since she was a little girl. She has always been too good for this little town and the people in it. I learned a long time ago that the best thing to do as far as Elizabeth is concerned is to just ignore her. Just let her go," her aunt stressed.

Mya clutched her hands at her sides, trying to release some of the pent-up anger coursing through her blood. Aunt Mo was right. Letting Elizabeth get on that plane was the best thing for all of them. Now they could focus on her grandmother.

"You have your own plane to catch, don't you?" Aunt Mo asked.

"I'm not going anywhere until I know Grandma is okay. I can spare some time off," Mya continued when she saw her aunt about to protest. "I'm between shows right now, and anything else I need to do can be accomplished via email."

Maureen shrugged her shoulders as they exited the privacy room. "I won't waste my

46

time arguing. Lord knows you're just as stubborn as Elizabeth."

Mya gasped. "You would compare me to *that* woman?" She put her hand to her chest as if covering a wound. "Now that's just mean, Aunt Mo."

As soon as they reentered the waiting room, Corey shot up from his seat. "Is everything okay? I came back from Drusilla's and you were both gone."

"The doctor took us to another room to update us on Mama's status," Aunt Mo answered. "She's fine, but they want to keep her to run additional tests."

Mya saw the way his shoulders wilted with relief and she was struck again by this complete one-eighty. Fifteen years ago, Corey Anderson was enemy number one in her grandmother's eyes. She'd claimed he was only after one thing and had forbidden Mya to see him. It hadn't stopped her, of course. Mya had been intrigued; she had craved the taste of trouble.

As a cocky seventeen-year-old, Corey had done everything he could to live up to her grandmother's low expectations of him. He'd encouraged Mya to sneak out of the house at all hours of the night. He'd snuck liquor from his daddy's liquor cabinet and gotten her drunk on more than one occasion.

And let's not forget the biggest trouble of all — her brush with the stork.

Corey had never learned of the pregnancy and, as far as Mya knew, her grandmother still thought the two nights Mya had spent in the hospital was from a vicious stomach bug that had been going around. Aunt Mo was the only one who knew about the baby she'd miscarried at seven weeks. She doubted her grandmother and Corey would be so chummy now if either of them knew about *that* little incident.

Mya pushed back against the wave of shame that threatened to crash through her whenever she thought of the child she'd never told Corey about, and the heartache it still summoned. It was too long ago to even matter anymore.

Corey's cell phone trilled. He held up a finger and answered. "Yeah? . . . Tell me you're lying. . . . Damn." He pocketed the phone. "I need to go."

"That's fine, honey," Aunt Mo said, giving him a hug. "Thanks for bringing Mya."

Her aunt turned to her. "They'll probably put Mama in her own room soon, so I'm going to run back to the house to get some clothes, and then come back here for the

48

night. They'll only let one family member stay, though."

"I know," Mya answered. "I'll go home once visiting hours are over."

"What time do you want me to come back and pick you up?" Corey asked.

"I'll call Phil," Mya answered, knowing her best friend, Phylicia, would drop whatever she was doing to be at her side. "I don't plan to leave the hospital anytime soon anyway," Mya said. "Don't worry, I'll be fine."

A smile, subtle though it was, inched up the corner of his mouth. "No one ever doubted you'd be fine, Peaches." He kissed Aunt Mo on the cheek. "I'll see you later. You tell Mrs. Eloise not to scare us like that anymore."

Mya watched as Corey left the waiting room. She waited until she was sure he was out of earshot before turning to her aunt. "What's going on here?"

"What?" Aunt Mo asked.

If Mya didn't spend her life around the theater, she would have bought the innocent act. "Don't even try it," she said. "When did you, Corey and Grandma all become best friends? The two of you both hated him."

"We did not *hate* him," her aunt protested.

"At least I didn't. I was just concerned that he was a bit too fast for you. With good reason," her aunt added with a pointed look. "But all of that is beside the point. Corey's not the boy he was when you two were in high school."

"How do you know that? He's been gone from Gauthier nearly as long as I have."

"That's not entirely true," her aunt said. "Corey visited several times a year when his daddy was still living. He moved back last year to coach the high school baseball team."

"You still haven't explained why he's all of a sudden your new BFF," Mya said.

"My what?"

"Forget it." Mya sighed. "I just think it's strange. Grandma thought those Anderson boys were nothing but trouble back when I was in high school, and now she's got one cutting her grass? Why didn't she ever mention him when I called home?"

Her aunt hunched her shoulders. "Maybe she didn't think it was a big deal to you. As far as Mama is concerned, everything between you and Corey ended after you graduated from high school."

"It *did* end after graduation," Mya stated. "Still . . ."

Was there a "still"? Corey was nothing

more than a guy she'd dated a long time ago. It had been years since she'd seen him, since she'd had anything to do with him. Why should it matter after all these years that he'd moved back to town and ingratiated himself to her family?

A nurse entered the waiting room. "Dubois family?"

"Right here," Mya called. She and Aunt Mo sprung from their seats like coils in a new mattress. "How is she?" Mya asked the nurse.

"She's doing well. She's in room seventeen. Follow me — I'll take you to her."

CHAPTER 3

Corey pulled into an empty parking spot between two Gauthier P.D. cruisers. He noticed his friend Jamal's shiny silver-and-black quad cab parked a couple of spaces down. He walked through the front doors of the brick building and was greeted by Manny Gilbert. Manny, who had spent his last two years of high school as shortstop for the Gauthier Fighting Lions baseball team, was now a cop.

"Where are they?" was Corey's greeting.

"In the back. We left them in the cell."

"Good," Corey said. "Safer for them to have bars between us."

"Don't be too hard on them. We did much worse when we were on the team."

"Yeah, well, I wasn't coaching the team back then. Any stupid crap they get into reflects on me."

By the time they reached the cell area, Corey could feel the vein in the middle of his forehead throbbing. The three knuckle-heads sat shoulder to shoulder on a bench inside the cell. Jamal Johnson stood just outside the cell door.

He and Jamal had been friends for years, ever since they'd played collegiate ball together. Jamal had decided to make Gauthier his new home earlier this year, and he had offered to help Corey out with the baseball team since the school district had turned down Corey's request to hire another assistant coach.

"So they called you first?" Corey asked Jamal.

His friend shrugged. "Guess they thought I'd go easier on them."

He nodded toward Manny, then stood to the side as the man disengaged the lock. Corey stepped into the holding cell, bracing his feet apart and crossing his arms over his chest.

"You three really thought I wouldn't hear about this?"

"Sorry, Coach," they said in unison.

"What did they do to the house?" Corey directed his question to Jamal.

"Took the porch light out with a BB gun. Covered a few of the windows with black paint. Pissed on the back steps."

"Junior high stuff," Corey snorted, shaking his head. He turned to Manny, who had taken the spot next to Jamal outside of the cell. "How long are they in here for?"

"Coach!" Terrence Smith, his star outfielder, jumped up from the bench. "You can't leave us here."

"You did the crime, didn't you?" Corey fired at him.

"And you were stupid enough to get caught," Jamal added.

"We were just playing around," Terrence maintained.

"By vandalizing the assistant principal's house? You three couldn't think of anything better to do?"

"They're lucky Donaldson is out of town. He would demand you three be locked up," Manny said.

"But, Coach, you can't leave us in here. This'll look bad to the scouts," Pierre Jones, the centerfielder, said.

"Maybe you should have thought about that before you decided to act like a bunch of children instead of young men on their way to college next year." Corey bore down on them, backing them to the bench. "You think you'll be able to get away with stunts like this at LSU, or Tulane, or Alabama?" he roared at Andre Thomas, the pitcher and best player on the team. "They'll kick you out of there so fast you won't know what's hit you."

"I know, Coach," Terrence said.

"We're sorry," Pierre added.

Corey knew he'd gotten his point across when they all crouched back. He noticed Andre Thomas's chin remained defiantly stiff.

The boy's recalcitrance incensed Corey even further. He had no doubt Andre had been the ringleader. The kid seemed hell-bent on causing as much trouble as he could around town. He had so much potential, but was flushing it down the toilet because he was more concerned with being a knuckle-head. Corey refused to sit back and watch Andre ruin his future.

He cut another menacing glare at his players and stepped out of the holding cell. "It's your call, Officer Gilbert."

Manny glanced his way, and Corey knew they were on the same wavelength.

"Well, you know we don't play favorites," Manny said in his best take-no-crap police-officer voice. "Just because these guys are baseball players doesn't mean they can get off scot-free."

Despite the seriousness of the situation, Corey had to bite back a laugh. He and Manny had gotten away with more than they should have back in the day. Partly because Manny's dad had been the police chief. The entire squad used to cut them slack, especially if they were playing Kentwood or Jesuit. Nothing got in the way of a big game against a known rival.

Jamal leaned to the side and whispered to Corey, "We're not really leaving them in here, are we?"

"Hell no," Corey whispered back. "We're in the middle of the season.

"So, Officer Gilbert," he called. "What'll it be?"

The trio of hefty ballplayers looked as if they'd shrunk five inches over the past ten minutes. They sat hunched over. Corey was pretty sure Pierre Jones was trembling.

"They're all still minors, right?" Manny asked.

"Yeah," Corey answered.

"Since this is a first offense for all three . . ." Manny paused. One by one, the boys' heads rose, as if sensing hope. "I'll let them off with a warning. I'll leave their punishment up to you."

The three collapsed with relief, glancing at each other with conspiratorial grins.

"You three really think you just got the easier end of the bargain, don't you?" Corey asked with deliberate softness as he stepped back into the cell. He closed the gap between them, bending down to eye level with his players before continuing. "By the end of the week, you'll beg Officer Gilbert to let you back in here."

The grins vanished.

Corey stood and jerked his head toward the open cell door. All three shot out of the cell so fast, one would have thought they were sleek marathoners instead of bulky baseball players.

As he walked out of the cell, Manny and Jamal were both trying like hell to hold in their grins, neither doing a good job of it. Manny broke first. "Man, you learned more from Coach Edwards than I thought you did."

"I was channeling him for a bit there," Corey said. He turned to Jamal. "You'll never meet a hard ass like our old coach."

"Worse than Richards back when we were at Arizona State?" Jamal asked.

"Richards didn't have a thing on Edwards."

"He was a mean SOB." Manny shook his head.

"But he saved my life," Corey interjected. "If not for Edwards, I would probably be sitting in this jail, or in prison with Shawn and Stefan. I owe that old man everything."

"I'm glad you came back to coach." Manny clapped him on the shoulder. "That guy they brought in after Edwards retired wasn't worth the starched khaki pants he used to model around in."

"Some of the people around here wouldn't agree with you on that one," Corey reminded his ex-teammate. "In fact, I should probably sneak out the back door. If anyone sees me leaving here, news of my arrest will be the talk of the town by the end of the day."

Manny just shook his head, but didn't refute Corey's claim. Corey knew it was because he spoke the truth. If he hadn't been on national television and in sports magazines, half the people in this town would have probably thought he'd been in jail instead of playing in the major league. With good reason. He was, after all, one of those Anderson boys.

Because his eldest brother, Leon, was eight years older, he had avoided the stigma the twins had brought upon their family. Leon had been admired by many in Gauthier after he'd enlisted in the army straight out of high school, but the twins had wreaked havoc on this town. And since Corey was only a year younger than Stefan and Shawn, he'd quickly fallen in with his rowdy brothers.

Vandalism, breaking and entering, petty larceny, even taking Assistant Principal Donaldson's car for a joyride — he'd done it all. Now that he was back in Gauthier, Corey was determined to show the town that he'd changed.

"Is there any paperwork to fill out?" he asked Manny.

"I didn't process them."

"Maybe they can clean up the mess they made of Donaldson's house before he gets back," Jamal said.

"I'd leave it there," Manny grunted. "Serves him right for being such an idiot."

"It's been fifteen years." Corey chuckled. "You need to let that stuff go. I have."

"Let it go, my ass," Manny mumbled.

"During our freshman year, Donaldson caught a bunch of us smoking behind the gymnasium," Corey explained to Jamal. "He suspended us all for a week, but Manny got two weeks because he was the one who brought the cigarettes. Ever since then, the two of them have butted heads."

Terrence, Andre and Pierre were waiting at the booking counter. Corey got back into character as he approached the boys. "When you leave here, go straight to Donaldson's house. I want every window spotless, and not just the ones you painted. And you all better work fast, because you don't know what time I'll be there to inspect. You got me?"

Three heads bobbed in unison.

Corey turned and nodded at Manny, flashing his friend a knowing smile before leaving the station.

"How long you going to give them to clean the place up?" Jamal asked as they headed for their vehicles.

Corey shrugged. "I'll swing by sometime tomorrow. I really don't care what they did to Donaldson's house. Manny's right, the guy is an idiot."

Jamal chuckled. "Gotta love a place where the police let you exact revenge."

"Don't mistake him for being a pushover. Manny can be hard-core when he needs to be. His dad was tough. He busted me and my two brothers more times than I can count."

Soon after Jamal told him of his plans to move to Gauthier, Corey had clued him in on his family's history in the town. Knowing the way folks here gossiped, Corey figured his friend would be regaled with stories of Decker Anderson's troublemaking sons within ten minutes of his arrival anyway.

They reached Jamal's truck first. "So, now that you don't have to play bad-ass baseball coach anymore, you think you can swing by and help me with some sanding? I'm trying to refinish the banister on the front staircase."

"Didn't I warn you against buying that run-down house?" Corey laughed.

Jamal — an architect by trade — had bought a fixer-upper in the old part of Gauthier. Corey had tried to talk him into buying a house in one of the newer subdivisions, but Jamal said he hadn't moved to a small town just to live in a house that looked as if it belonged in the city. Corey figured his friend was regretting that decision after losing his first several months in town to renovations.

"Don't talk about my house, man." Jamal punched him on the shoulder. "The work is going better than I thought. You think you can lend me a hand later today?"

An image of Mya's distraught face flashed in his mind. Corey shook his head. "I'll be tied up for the rest of the day. Maybe you should just get a professional over there. Why don't you call Phil?"

"Who's Phil?"

"One of the most talented home restoration specialists you'll ever meet." Corey

61

pulled out his wallet and searched. "I thought I had a business card, but apparently not. Just do an internet search for Phillips' Home Restoration."

"You sure this Phil is good?" Jamal asked. "I want to make sure that banister is preserved. I need this done right."

"Don't worry." Corey smiled. "You won't be sorry with Phil."

They bumped fists, then Corey headed for his SUV. He'd wanted to get a couple of projects done at his own place this weekend, but it looked as though he'd have to push those to the side for now. Starting up the Escalade, Corey pulled onto the street and headed for the Dubois house.

Mya waited at the four-way stop sign at the corner of Water Street and Pecan Drive as a line of kids on bicycles crossed the street. A straggler pedaled up to the edge of the curb. Mya waved him along, grinning as his little legs pumped to catch up with his friends.

She cranked up the air conditioner in Aunt Mo's car and continued along Pecan Drive, on this all-important errand for her grandmother. The stately homes that lined the broad avenue stood like elegant Southern belles. Their well-kept yards were surrounded by short, wooden picket fences, while others had graduated to the vinyl fencing Mya would love to have installed out at her grandparents'.

Grandma had labeled this neighborhood pretentious, based on the fact that its residents were not allowed to grow vegetables in their backyards. Mya didn't care how uptight they were. She used to love walking through this area on her way to work at Gauthier Pharmacy and Feed Store, imagining what it must be like to live in what had seemed like mansions to her young, unworldly mind.

Pecan Drive turned into Main Street after the intersection at Pecan and Shoal Creek Lane. As she cruised down Main, Mya was once again struck by how much everything looked the same. It was as if time had stopped.

Main Street had always been this town's pride and joy. Back when she'd worked here after school, every proprietor had been required to sign an agreement stating that they would paint their storefronts every year. Littering had been a dirty word, and the Gauthier police department had responded to a call for loitering just as fast as one for shoplifting.

Mya pulled into a slanted parking spot in front of Claudette's Beauty Parlor. Like the rest of the buildings on Main, Claudette's looked as if it had been lifted from a painting entitled *Small-Town Life.*

She headed up the wooden steps that led to the wraparound porch. The beauty shop shared a porch with Lou Cannon's Dry Cleaning and the Main Street Sweet Shop. Across the street was the pharmacy, post office and Emile's Restaurant, Gauthier's version of five-star dining.

Mya walked through the door of the beauty shop and smiled in remembrance as the familiar sounds and smells greeted her.

"Hello, everybody," she called.

"Well, look who decided to step into my shop." Claudette Robinson set down a curling iron and stepped from behind a salon chair, embracing Mya in a long hug.

"I'm sorry we didn't get a chance to talk after the funeral," Mya apologized.

"Don't you worry about that," Claudette said, adding an extra squeeze before letting Mya go. "There were so many people at the house, it was impossible to visit with everybody. How is Eloise doing? Did the doctor say when she'd be out of the hospital?"

"She should be home tomorrow. Monday at the latest," Mya said.

"I knew something was wrong when she didn't show up for her hair appointment this morning, especially since she knew her new wig was in. She's been waiting for it for over a month. Deena is finishing it up right now."

Mya spotted the young girl standing before the mannequin, a comb in one hand, a spray bottle in the other. She spritzed the salt-and-pepper wig and teased the tight curls out of their stubborn position.

"She's laid up in a hospital bed. You would think she'd have other things on her mind," Mya said.

"When the new wig she's been waiting for is at my shop?" Claudette looked at her as if she were crazy. "That New York air has addled your mind, girl. I'm surprised Eloise didn't order the paramedics to swing by on their way to the hospital."

"If she were conscious, believe me, she would have." Mya laughed.

Deena came over with her grandmother's new wig, and Mya thanked her with a ten-dollar tip.

"You tell Eloise I'll try to get over to the house once they let her out of that hospital," Claudette said. "And tell her not to worry about the meeting Monday night. I'll make sure Margery doesn't go overboard."

"You all have a deaconess board meeting?" Mya asked.

"No, that's on Wednesday nights," Claudette said. "This is for the civic association. A group of us started it a couple of years ago. Your grandmother is head of the committee for the town's 175th-year celebration. She didn't tell you?"

Mya shook her head. "We haven't had much time to talk about anything outside of Granddad's funeral."

Claudette's smile sobered.

"I'm sure she'll appreciate you keeping Mrs. Margery in line," Mya said. "It was good seeing you again, Claudette."

"You too, honey." Claudette winked as she returned to her customer.

Mya left the beauty shop and climbed back into the car, careful not to smash the curls as she placed the freshly styled wig on the passenger seat. She put the key in the ignition, but her hand halted when she looked up and saw the pharmacy in the rearview mirror. She got out of the car and, with a quick glance from left to right, crossed the two-way street and took a step back in time.

The same bell that had hung above the door when she'd last walked out of it chimed Mya's entrance into the pharmacy. She'd worked the entire summer before her senior year, her plans for leaving Gauthier already firm in her mind. She'd saved up enough for first and last month's rent and a plane ticket out of town.

The store hadn't changed a bit. Next to the door was a hat and umbrella stand, and directly across from the front entrance was a display of the handmade soaps and lotions Mrs. Landry, the pharmacist's wife, made in her kitchen. Mya picked up four bars of lemon verbena. God, that scent brought back memories.

She strolled down the aisle, picking up a few toiletries, extra moisturizer and a razor. Since she'd planned to be in Gauthier for only a couple of days she hadn't bothered to bring most of this stuff.

Mya took her purchases to the counter, but stopped short as she noticed the woman standing behind the counter.

"Shelly?" Mya asked with a tentative step forward.

The woman blinked several times. "Mya? Oh, my goodness. How are you, girl?"

"I'm fine," Mya said, trying to suppress the shock in her voice. "How are you doing?" Though what she really wanted to ask was "What are you doing?"

Shelly Hunt had graduated valedictorian of their high school class. Granted, it was a class of only seventy-eight students, but

67

even so, Shelly had been destined for great things. She'd received full-ride scholarships to several universities. What was she doing working behind the counter at the pharmacy? Unless she'd bought it? Maybe she'd become a pharmacist?

Please, let that be the case.

"So, did Dr. Landry finally retire?" Mya asked, placing her items on the counter.

"Yeah, right. That man doesn't know what retirement means." Shelly laughed. "He's having lunch over at Emile's." She rang up the soap. "I'm really sorry I couldn't make your grandfather's funeral yesterday. I had to take my youngest to the doctor. Turned out to be just a stomach bug, but you never know with the little ones. You have any kids?" Shelly asked.

Mya shook her head. "Nope, it's just me."

"Sometimes I wish." Shelly grinned as she handed Mya the bag. "I have three. My oldest is trying out for the varsity baseball team, so if you talk to Corey, tell him to take it easy on my baby."

"I will," Mya said. "How old is he?"

"Almost fifteen," Shelly answered.

"Wow, so you were pregnant when we graduated? I had no clue."

"No one did, until the truth got too hard to hide." Shelly chuckled, making a round-ing motion over her belly. "I had Devon that September."

"All this time I thought you'd started at Dillard University the fall after we graduated," Mya said.

"I tried after Devon was born, but then I got pregnant with Angelica." Shelly shrugged. "It just never worked out, and eventually they pulled the scholarship they offered me."

Mya's heart lurched at the regret that flashed across Shelly's face. "Well, you know what they say, 'It's never too late.' "

"Yeah, right." Shelly waved off the idea. "Can you imagine me in someone's classroom? I'll just make sure my little ones go on to college. Besides, Dr. Landry couldn't run this place without me."

"You're probably right. I remember how scatter-brained he could be." They shared a laugh. "Well, it was great seeing you again, Shelly."

"You, too."

By the time she walked out of the door, Mya could hardly breathe, so haunted was she by the fate she'd managed to escape. It was a travesty that someone with so much promise could end up working as the check-out girl at a small-town pharmacy.

That could have been you, a voice whispered in her head.

As she drove back to the hospital, Mya tried to imagine what her life would have been like if she had remained in Gauthier. The thought was so disturbing her mind refused to conjure a single image. Instead, a picture of her two-story Brooklyn apartment, with its exposed-brick walls, hardwood floors and view of lower Manhattan, traced across her mind's eye. She visualized the diverse faces she passed as she went about her day in the city. The hodgepodge of ethnicities and cultures that had added such richness to her life was the antithesis of these same faces from her childhood.

Thank God this place hadn't managed to get its hooks into her.

As the thought floated through her mind, Mya felt an uncomfortable mixture of shame and guilt stir in the pit of her stomach. It was unfair to lay all the blame at the town's feet. Her actions fifteen years ago made her just as culpable in the trap that had nearly snared her.

Mya pulled into the parking lot and, grabbing her grandmother's wig from the front seat, made her way to her grandmother's hospital room. She learned that Grandma had been moved to another room on the hospital's west side. Following the signs in the white, sterile hallways, Mya found her grandmother's room.

She tapped lightly on the partially open door as she entered. "Knock, knock," she called. The room was outfitted in much the same way as the previous one, but instead of two beds, the other half of the room contained two reclining chairs and a small table.

"Bring me my hair," her grandmother said.

She walked over to the bed and handed her grandmother the wig. "Why did they have to move you?" Mya asked.

"They didn't *have* to move her," Aunt Mo drawled, coming out of the bathroom that Mya hadn't noticed tucked behind the door. "But putting her in a private room was easier than arguing with her."

"Are you making trouble already?" Mya gave her grandmother a stern look.

"My roommate snored," she answered, fluffing the wig's tight curls. "It looks even better in person. Here, help me get this on."

Mya removed the hairpins and lifted the old wig from her grandmother's head, replacing it with the one she'd just brought. "Claudette hasn't changed a bit," she laughed, tucking a curl behind her grandmother's ear.

"Did you expect her to? She's been the same way since we were in the sixth grade," her grandmother answered.

Mya chuckled. "She said something about a meeting Monday night?"

"Oh, dammit," Grandma cursed.

"Mama!" Aunt Mo screeched.

"Oh, calm down, Maureen. You'd think she's never heard a dirty word before," her grandmother griped. "They've got to let me out of this hospital. I need to be at that meeting Monday night."

"That's up to your doctor," Mya said. "Claudette said you're in charge of some celebration committee?"

Her grandmother straightened her shoulders. "I'm chairing the committee for the town's 175th-year anniversary and the downtown revitalization project, which *some* people think is a waste of time."

"She means Margery," Aunt Mo said.

"I don't care what Margery thinks. We need to do something," her grandmother argued.

Mya folded her arms across her chest. "Grandma, what are you up to?"

"It's not just me," she said with an affronted pout. She pointed an accusing finger at Mya's chest. "It's that darn outlet mall in Maplesville that's causing problems.

That's where everyone shops now, and what's worse, the people who built the outlet mall have their sights set on Main Street. They're trying to bring in one of those big-box stores. Can you imagine what would happen to the businesses on Main if they had to compete with a huge national chain?"

"So you came up with the idea for an anniversary celebration?"

"Yes." Her grandmother nodded. "We figure the celebration will draw people back to Main Street and show those developers that we don't need some megastore moving in. But how am I supposed to get any work done laid up in this hospital bed?"

"Should have thought about that when you ate all that cake yesterday," Maureen said.

"Would you take her back to New York with you?" Grandma asked.

"I'm not sure New York can handle Aunt Mo for more than a week at a time." Mya laughed. "Besides, I'm not going back just yet. I'm going to stay for a few days, just to make sure you're okay."

The grateful smile that came over her grandmother's face sent a bolt of shame careening through Mya's chest. Her decision to remain in town an extra couple of days should not have been a big deal, but her grandmother's joy at the announcement spoke a truth that was hard for Mya to face.

If her grandmother had expected her to leave while she was lying in a hospital bed, Mya must be just a step above Elizabeth in Grandma's eyes.

"I have a wonderful idea." Her grandmother squeezed her hand. "You can go to the meeting in my place Monday night!"

A tight ball of *Please, don't make me!* ricocheted against the walls of Mya's chest. It's not as if she had plans for the time she would spend in Gauthier — she wasn't even supposed to *be* in Gauthier this long. But Mya could think of a thousand things she'd rather do than spend a Monday night with a group of her grandmother's contemporaries.

"Grandma . . ." Mya groaned.

"Oh, Mya, please. We only have a month left, and there's so much work to do. I need to know what they talk about."

"But Claudette said she'll let you know," she tried.

Her grandmother waved her off. "Claudette hardly pays attention. She's always too busy gossiping, as if she doesn't do enough of that in her shop all day."

Mya stared at the instruments above the

bed so she wouldn't have to see the entreaty on her grandmother's face.

"If you don't go, I'll just have to go myself. I'll drag all these machines with me if I have to. And if I happen to pass out again . . ." She shrugged her shoulders.

"You are *so* not playing fair right now," Mya accused her. "Aunt Mo, tell her." Mya looked to her aunt for support, but Maureen kept her eyes on the crossword puzzle in her hands. Mya noticed the faint smile tipping up the corner of her lips.

She shook her head, accepting defeat. "Fine," Mya said. "I'll go to the meeting."

Her grandmother reached over and patted her hand. "I knew you'd do the right thing. Now, go to the house and look on the bureau in my room. I have a green binder with all my notes. You need to look over them before the meeting. And don't you let Clementine Washington bring up that magic show again. I told that woman nobody is going to come downtown to see her grandson perform magic tricks. He's not that good anyway."

"No magic," Mya said with a sharp nod.

"And take out that corn bread casserole I have in the freezer for dinner tomorrow."

"Don't worry about dinner." Mya brushed off her suggestion. "I'll probably just open a can of soup and make a sandwich."

"Corey will not be satisfied with soup and a sandwich."

"Why do I have to worry about what he wants?"

"Because he always comes over for Sunday dinner," her grandmother answered, as if having the boy she once ran off her porch with a broomstick over for dinner was no big deal. Apparently, it *wasn't* a big deal to anyone but Mya.

This new dynamic between her family and Corey was hard to comprehend.

"Mama, Corey knows you're in the hospital. I doubt he's expecting Sunday dinner," Maureen reasoned.

"Just to be on the safe side, you take out that casserole and cook some greens to go with it. You remember how to make greens, don't you?" Her grandmother asked.

"Yeah, sure," Mya answered. Though she wasn't about to cook greens or anything else for Corey. She placed a kiss on her grandmother's forehead. "Don't worry about anything at the house, or at the meeting. You just concentrate on getting better. And don't give the hospital staff a hard time."

Aunt Mo huffed a laugh.

"Oh, shut up, Maureen," her grandmother said. "Will I see you tomorrow?" she asked

Mya. "After you go to church, of course," she added.

Mya groaned but nodded before leaving the hospital room. She called her best friend from high school, Phylicia Phillips, who happened to be ten minutes away. Phylicia arrived in a blue pickup, a magnetic sign publicizing Phillips' Home Restoration on the door.

She honked the horn, leaning an elbow on the edge of the open window. "Get your butt in here, girl."

Mya bounded up to the truck and climbed in. "Thanks for picking me up, Phil."

"No problem," Phylicia said, her radiant smile and envy-worthy face clashing with her well-worn overalls. The smudge of dirt on her high cheekbone didn't detract from her appeal one bit.

"Sorry I didn't make it to the house after the funeral," Phil said. "I had to get back to work. I'm on a tight deadline with this project."

"You never told me what it is you're doing."

"I'm working on the Rosedale Plantation," Phil answered with the kind of lustful sigh one employed when talking about a lover.

Mya laughed at the pure ecstasy on her friend's face. "You must be in heaven."

"You have no idea how long I've wanted to get my hands on that house."

Phylicia's dad, Percy Phillips, was the original Phil, but the nickname and the restoration business had passed down to Phylicia when her father died. Phil had expanded the business, catering to special restoration projects across the South.

As they drove back to her grandparents' place, Mya filled her in on her grandmother's condition. She was about to ask Phil what she knew about Corey's relationship with her family when they pulled up to the house and she spotted his Escalade parked next to the mailbox.

Mya's eyes roamed around the yard, and then grew wide. Corey Anderson, shirtless and sweaty, was picking up the vegetables that had fallen to the ground in her grandfather's garden.

"Good Lord," Phylicia breathed. "Is it safe to leave you here?"

Mya wasn't so sure, but she answered, "Of course. That thing between Corey and I happened a long time ago, Phil. I'm over him."

Phylicia slid her that unconvinced look that hadn't changed since high school.

"Oh, whatever," Mya said, opening the door and sliding out of the truck. "Thanks for the ride. We're going to get together before I leave, right?"

"Just tell me when and where," Phil said. She motioned to the garden with her chin. Mya glanced over her shoulder and found Corey standing next to the stalks of corn, watching them. Phil's brows rose and one corner of her mouth hitched up in a smile. "Good luck," she said with a little wave before driving off.

Mya took a deep, fortifying breath before turning and heading toward the naked chest she'd dreamt about for a solid five years after leaving Gauthier.

CHAPTER 4

Corey carried the bushel overflowing with mustard greens and sat it on the back porch, then picked up another of the wooden baskets and headed back toward the garden. He could feel the blood rushing faster in his veins as he neared Mya, who had stopped just at the edge of the garden, next to the tomato patch.

"I see you finished cutting the grass." She motioned to the lawn he'd finished trimming an hour ago, before pulling the weeds from the front flower bed. After he was done with the weeds, he'd started on the garden. He kept telling himself he was just being a good neighbor. He hadn't been finding things to do just so he could stick around until Mya came home.

"How's Mrs. Eloise doing?" Corey asked.

"Stubborn as ever and causing the hospital staff all kinds of grief."

"That's my girl." Corey laughed.

After a beat, Mya tilted her head to the side and asked, "Since when?"

The curiosity in her voice was expected, but he was thrown by the unease coloring the simple question. Was the fact that he got along with her grandmother a sign of the apocalypse? He'd thought — rather, he'd hoped — that she would be pleased about the way things were between him and her family.

"Things change, Mya. People change." He wiped the sweat from his brow with the back of his hand. "Do you have a problem with me getting along with your family?"

"No. It's just . . . I don't know . . . different." She rubbed her arms as if she were chilly, despite the fact that they were smack in the middle of a ninety-degree day. "But I guess you're right. Things change."

Corey moved past her and started picking ripened tomatoes from the vines. Mya bent over the stalk a couple of feet away and plucked several tomatoes.

"On the other hand, some things never change," she said. "I was just on Main Street. Felt as if I'd stumbled into a time machine."

"It's been that way for as long as I can remember. Had you expected anything different?" Corey asked.

81

"I guess not. Though, according to Grandma, support for the businesses on Main has been dwindling because of the new outlet mall in Maplesville. She strong-armed me into attending a meeting Monday night with her civic association. They're trying to revitalize downtown Gauthier and stop some big-box store from setting up shop."

Corey's back stiffened at the mention of Monday night's meeting. Should he tell her it was marked on his calendar, too, since he was the association's parliamentarian? He decided to keep his mouth shut. If she was going to the meeting, she'd find out soon enough.

"Actually, I think the new store is a good idea," he said instead. "It'll bring in jobs and additional tax revenue."

Mya's brow dipped in a slight frown. "It'll also hurt the surrounding businesses," she said. "Those mom-and-pop shops along Main Street add to Gauthier's charm. If you allow some national chain to come in, then Main Street will start to resemble your average strip mall."

"Mya, one of the reasons this town hasn't grown is because people think it's still stuck in the past. I've spoken with the developer —"

"You have?"

He nodded. "I'm considering becoming an investor. I've seen their plans, which are still in the very early stages, I should point out. I really think this could be a huge plus for Gauthier."

"Corey, if you want to put your money into this town, then invest in the businesses that are already here."

"Those family-run businesses have been here for ages. They're not the key to growing this community."

"And some generic chain store is?" Mya shook her head. "I'm with Grandma and her civic organization on this one. I think this new development would harm Gauthier more than help. It'll be interesting to hear what they've come up with at the meeting Monday night."

"I didn't think you'd be in town long enough to attend their meeting," Corey said.

She shrugged a shoulder. "I've decided to stay for another few days, at least until Grandma is out of the hospital. I'm between shows right now, so I can spare the time off."

The thought of Mya remaining in Gauthier caused his pulse to race and his chest to tighten with a painfully sweet ache. He felt like a seventeen-year-old kid again, getting excited because the girl he liked had bothered to look his way.

"I was told I have to cook Sunday dinner for you." Mya shot him a look that clearly said she'd rather strap on a pair of waders and go searching for frogs in the swamp.

"Don't worry about it." Corey laughed. "I figured Sunday dinner was off since Mrs. Eloise is in the hospital. I made other plans."

"You did?"

The subtle inquiry in her voice brought Corey's head up. She quickly turned her attention back to the tomatoes, but not before he caught the brief uncertainty that flashed in her eyes. The thought that she was even the slightest bit interested in how — or rather *with whom* — he was spending his Sunday felt damn good.

"I promised my buddy Jamal that I'd help with some house renovations," Corey said, overcome by a sudden urge to ease her mind. "He bought one of the old houses on Pecan Drive and has been doing all the work himself, though I told him to call Phil to help with one project."

"I think she's on her way over there now. She told me she was headed to that part of town."

Mya moved to the tomato plant next to the one he was working on, and her arm brushed against his. Corey sucked in a quick breath. The brief contact felt like fire against his skin.

"Good," Corey managed to get out. He swallowed hard and pulled in another deep lungful of air. "I was afraid he would try to do the work himself." He shot Mya a quick grin. "Now, if you start feeling domestic tomorrow, we won't turn down lunch. You can bring it over to Jamal's."

"I think you'd better pack a sandwich," Mya said. A bit of that sass returning to her smile, she tossed a tomato into his bushel. "Here, I'll even provide the tomato."

Corey shook his head. "You've still got a smart mouth on you, Peaches." She cut her eyes at him, and Corey realized his mistake. "Sorry," he said. "It's hard to think of you as Mya."

"Try harder," she said. She emptied the tomatoes she'd collected into his bushel, then reached over and picked it up. Propping the basket on her hip, she turned and started toward the house. Over her shoulder she said, "Thanks for helping with the garden, but you can leave now. I'll take care of the rest of these tomorrow."

Corey stood between the rows of vegetables, staring at Mya's backside as she climbed the porch steps and entered the house. How one woman could possess so much audaciousness was beyond him, but he had to admit he was happy she would be around to flaunt it awhile longer. If there was one thing he could count on, it was that he would never be bored when Mya was around.

Corey parked behind Jamal's truck and lifted the beat-up leather tool belt from the passenger seat. It was his father's. Corey felt a stab of pride every time he used it.

He walked along the side of the huge Georgian. According to Jamal, the house had been unoccupied for years before he bought it, but you'd never know by looking at it. The outside of the house was in pristine condition.

The inside was a different story. Over the past six months, Jamal had completely gutted it. His friend had some wild ideas when it came to incorporating green technology into older structures. The original owners were probably turning in their graves at the changes Jamal had made to the place.

Corey rounded the house and found Jamal hunched over a sawhorse, splitting a board of plywood with a table saw. He waited until the whirl of the saw had quieted before speaking.

"Looks as if things are going good," Corey greeted him.

Jamal looked up with pure murder shining in eyes that were covered with safety goggles.

Corey held his hands up in surrender. "What did I do to get the death glare?"

"It's what you *didn't* do," Jamal said. "You could have tipped me off about Phil."

"What about Phil?" Corey asked, trying like hell to keep a straight face as he hooked the tool belt around his waist.

"Don't give me that innocent crap," Jamal groused. "You could have told me Phil was a woman — one who looks like a damn swimsuit model."

Corey couldn't hold back his grin any longer. "I didn't even think about it," he lied. "I went to high school with Phylicia. She's always looked like a swimsuit model, even when she's dressed in those baggy overalls. Did she do a good job with your wood?"

Jamal's glower was lethal.

"Sorry." Corey laughed. "That was too good to pass up. Seriously, will Phil be able to help? I know her business keeps her pretty busy."

"She's pretty bossy is what she is," Jamal said. "She chewed me out because I removed the paneling from the entryway. Told me I was destroying this house. I had to keep reminding her that it is *my* house."

Corey barked out a laugh. "Sounds like Phil. She gets passionate about this stuff."

Jamal mumbled something under his breath. Looking up at the sky, he said, "If this rain holds out long enough for me to get all these boards cut, I might get the floors in the bathroom done today. Then I'll just have to lay down the ceramic tile."

"You know, Phil does a good job with flooring, too." Corey held his hands up when Jamal shot him another of those looks. "I'm just messing with you."

Corey dodged the wood chip Jamal pitched at his head and set about sanding the baseboards for the bathroom. Hours passed as they worked in silence with only the radio playing from a boom box, circa 1992, and the occasional roll of thunder rumbling in the distance. Despite the ominous clouds creeping in from the west, just enough sun shone down to make Corey's mouth water for one of the beers peeking out of the ice-filled metal bucket.

As if he'd read his mind, Jamal asked, "You ready for a break?"

Corey glanced at his sports watch. "It's about time for lunch. You feel like eating a po'boy from Mitchell's? I think they're open until two on Sundays."

"I still don't understand why people around here can't just call it a submarine sandwich like the rest of society," Jamal said.

"Because we do things differently down here, in case you haven't noticed," Corey said, pulling his wallet from his back pocket and checking to make sure he had enough cash for two sandwiches and a couple of bags of chips. Jamal tried to hand him a twenty, but Corey waved him off.

As he pocketed his money, Jamal's eyes focused on something over Corey's shoulder. He held up a hand. "Hi there."

Corey whipped around to find Mya walking toward them, carrying a foil-wrapped plate in each hand. She wore the same khaki capri pants and sleeveless shirt she'd changed into after her grandfather's funeral, but his heart started to race so fast one would think she was wearing a string bikini.

"Hi," Mya greeted them.

"You actually brought us lunch?" Corey asked.

She shrugged. "I've already visited Grandma, picked the rest of the ripe vegetables from the garden, swept the entire house and hung the bedsheets on the clothesline, although that was probably a mistake," she said, looking back at the gray clouds inching closer. "Grandma has no internet or cable, and the library is closed, so I can't even find a good book to read. Making lunch gave me something to do. You didn't tell me which house on Pecan. Good thing I spotted your SUV."

"I honestly didn't expect you to come by," Corey said. "Thank you."

"Yeah, thanks," Jamal said. "I'm Jamal, by the way." He relieved her of the plates and handed one to Corey. "You want a beer?" he asked Mya.

"No, thanks." She motioned toward the house. "You mind if I have a look? I've always wanted to see what this house looked like inside."

"Go ahead." Jamal nodded toward the open back door that led to what Jamal called a conversation room.

"I'll give you a tour," Corey offered. The food would be there when he got back. He wasn't sure how long Mya would be around.

She studied each and every feature as they methodically went from room to room. "I've always loved this house," Mya said, step- ping over the threshold of the arched door- way that led to the formal dining room. "I can't count the number of times I tripped on that bump in the sidewalk because I was so busy trying to catch a glimpse through the curtains as I walked to work."

"I know Jamal paid an arm and a leg for it, but he was determined to have this house."

"I'm surprised the family sold it. Most of these houses have been owned by the same families for generations."

Corey shrugged. "I guess the younger generation decided they didn't want small-town life. You know how that is, don't you?"

Her eyes narrowed in a reproachful glare. "I'm not the only one who left," she said.

"I came back," Corey challenged. "Even if it was just long enough to lay flowers on my parents' graves and stop in on a few of our friends from high school. I came back."

"I'm here now, aren't I?"

"But for how long?"

The air crackled between them like a charged wire. Mya held her chin stubbornly in the air, and all Corey could think to do was take it in his hand and tilt her face so he could kiss her. Desire pumped heavy and hot in his veins, the need to claim Mya a tangible thing.

Her chest rose on a deep, shuddering breath and her eyes dipped to his mouth. She ran the tip of her tongue along her bottom lip, and a low growl rumbled in his throat.

"Have you shown her what I did to the kitchen?" Jamal's yell from the hallway snapped the pull between them.

Mya was the first to look away, tearing her gaze from his and looking beyond his shoulder over to Jamal, who'd just stepped into the room.

"No, he hasn't," she said. "I'd love to see it." She dipped under and away from him, walking over to admire the wainscoting Jamal was pointing out. "You've done a great job here," Mya remarked.

"I haven't done it alone," Jamal said. He nodded toward Corey. "My man here has been right beside me for most of it. If baseball hadn't worked out for him, I think he would have made a good house builder."

Mya cut him a sly glance. "House builder, huh? I'm not sure if that fits the Corey Anderson I remember."

More like a house *robber.* Corey could practically hear her unspoken words.

As Jamal led the way to the kitchen, Corey hung back, assessing Mya.

The Corey Anderson she remembered was a bad boy who bucked authority and did his damnedest to mimic Shawn and Stefan, who had turned making mischief into an art form. Corey had been well on his way to a life of trouble, until Coach Edwards rescued him. But after being a hell-raiser for so long, it was hard to change people's minds.

He was determined to show the people of Gauthier that he had turned over a new leaf. Maybe in the process he could show Mya what she was missing out on. If Corey had anything to say about it, she wouldn't be so quick to run back to the big city. She had been away too long; he was going to remind her how great small-town life could be.

CHAPTER 5

As the steel door closed behind her, Mya was catapulted back to her past. Gauthier High School looked exactly the same, from the light green walls to the speckled vinyl tile flooring stretching from one end of the corridor to the other. It even *smelled* the same, like wax and lemon.

She walked with measured steps down the main hallway, her eyes wandering over framed photographs of various academic and social clubs throughout the years. She stopped in front of a picture of the National Beta Honor Society from her senior year and laughed out loud at her hairstyle. She'd spent a good portion of her weekly paycheck from the pharmacy buying the hair gel she used to keep those finger waves shellacked to her scalp.

A cackle of laughter resonated from the end of the hallway. Mya made her way to the home economics room where the civic association held their bimonthly meeting. She was instantly bombarded by people she'd just seen a few days ago at her grandfather's funeral, all conveying again how sorry they were about Big Harold's passing and inquiring about her grandmother's health. Claudette dragged her to a table with store-bought cookies and punch and insisted she have both.

"I saw Eloise today," Claudette said as she piled on the cookies. "She told me you were joining the committee."

Mya choked on her drink, shaking her head so vigorously punch sloshed out of her cup and onto her knuckle. "I'm not joining anything," she said. "I'm just here to take notes and report back to Grandma. She'll be out of the hospital and able to join you all soon."

"Whatever you say, honey." Claudette gave her a patronizing pat on the arm.

Before Mya could voice a rebuttal, Corey walked through the classroom door wearing a green polo shirt with *Gauthier Fighting Lions* embroidered on the left chest pocket.

"Sorry I'm late," he said. "Practice ran over."

Margery Lambert, who had been the head of the deaconess board at her childhood church for as long as Mya could remember, clapped her hands together and said, "Now that all the board members or their proxies are here, we can get started. As always, we will open with a prayer and ask God for special healing for Eloise Dubois, who can't be with us today."

Mya inched her way over toward Corey as Margery proved to the room just why she deserved her position as head deaconess.

"What are you doing here?" Mya asked in a fierce whisper.

"Shhh," Corey said. "We're supposed to be praying."

"Corey Anderson, don't stand there pretending you have a religious bone in your body. I know you."

The sexiest smile in the world pulled at the corner of his mouth, causing Mya's insides to turn into a melty puddle of goo.

The prayer ended and Margery passed out xeroxed copies of an agenda.

"What are you doing here?" Mya asked again.

"I'm a member of the civic association," he answered, that smirk broadening.

Yeah, right. Corey Anderson *so* did not fit in with this crowd.

As Margery ticked off items on the list, ranging from encouraging parish government to fill potholes around town to painting the benches in the park, Mya continued to hound him. "Stop playing around, Corey. What are you *really* doing here?"

He refused to answer her; he just continued to stare at the paper in his hand as if the meeting agenda had the most fascinating words ever written.

"What are we going to do about this new store that's trying to bully its way onto Main Street?" Barbara Cannon, whose husband owned Lou Cannon's Dry Cleaning, asked.

"Talk to him," Margery said, pointing at Corey. "He's the one who's trying to put everybody out of business."

"That is *not* what I'm trying to do," Corey said with an exasperated sigh. "Like I said at last month's meeting, the new developers are promising to work *with* the local businesses, not against them."

"That's what they say now," Claudette chimed in. "I stopped in at their Slidell location when I went to visit my daughter. They stock at least twenty national brands in their hair care section, all for less than what I can afford to sell them."

"Mrs. Claudette, people have been going to your shop for years. They're not going to stop because of this new store."

"They'll come to get their hair done, but they're going to go over to that new store to buy their hair spray. The money I make selling styling products pays my shop's utilities. You think I can do anybody's hair without electricity?"

Corey glanced over at Mya with a look that said *save me!*

She was tempted to let him suffer a bit longer, but it was evident that the room was becoming hostile. The grumblings were near a fever pitch.

"Why don't we revisit the issue regarding the new development later," Mya suggested. "If possible, I'd like to move the discussion to the downtown revitalization project."

"Oh, yes. I have some ideas."

Mya glanced to see who'd said that and barked out a nervous laugh as Clementine Washington waved her hand in the air.

"Actually," Mya interrupted, before Clementine could make any suggestions about her grandson pulling a rabbit out of a magical hat. "There is one thing I wanted to mention. As I was going through Grandma's notes, I couldn't help but notice that everything you all have planned for the revitalization project involves just the handful of people in this room."

"Well, we *are* the civic association," Margery said. "It's up to us to make sure stuff gets done around this town."

"You all can champion it, but you don't have to do it by yourselves," Mya pointed out. "Why don't you try getting the entire community more involved in the revitalization effort?"

Margery shot her a *well, duh* look. "That's what we're trying to do with the celebration."

"No, I mean before the celebration takes place. Why not get them involved in the preparation? Main Street is pretty well preserved, but when I was downtown earlier I noticed that there are bricks on the sidewalk that need to be replaced and those wrought-iron lampposts could use a new coat of paint. I'm sure you can get people to donate a few hours of their time to help spruce things up before the celebration."

"That's a good idea," Clementine said with a hint of awe, as if she was surprised Mya could come up with one of those.

"That's a *really* good idea," Corey agreed. "We can make it an organized event. I'll get the entire baseball team to pitch in. Gauthier High now requires students to earn fifty hours of community service before they graduate. I doubt most of them have reached that yet."

"The Lions Club can help, too," someone added.

"And the churches would certainly recruit people."

"Are you going to head this up, Mya?" Claudette asked.

"No." Mya shook her head. "I was just making the suggestion."

"Oh, I'll bet we can get supplies donated from the big hardware store in Maplesville," someone else said.

"We might as well clean up Heritage Park, too," another said.

"Mya, why don't you make a list of everything that we need."

Mya tried to protest again, but it was as if she were talking to a brick wall.

No doubt sensing her panic, Corey leaned over and whispered, "Don't worry. I'll work with you on this."

She slanted a glance his way and wasn't sure whether she should feel relieved or even more frightened at the thought of working with Corey on anything.

How had she ended up here? She should have been in her apartment in Brooklyn, eating a slice of pizza from the little restaurant down the block and watching reruns of *The Real Housewives of Atlanta.* Instead she'd just been volunteered to head up a committee to spruce up downtown Gauthier?

Mya felt the walls of the town closing in on her. And she couldn't do a single thing about it.

A half hour later, as she walked to Aunt Maureen's sedan, which was her new mode of transportation now that she'd returned her rental car, she was stopped by a hand to her shoulder. Mya jumped. She spun around, her hand flat on her chest.

"Sorry," Corey said. "I didn't mean to scare you."

"It's okay," she said with a relieved breath when she saw it was him.

"Thanks for saving me back in there," he said. "I'm pretty sure pitchforks were about to come out."

"I still think those women are right about the store," Mya stated.

He rolled his eyes and ticked items off on his fingers. "New jobs, greater selection of products, more sales tax revenues. Need I go on?"

Resting against the driver's-side door, she folded her arms across her chest and said, "Nothing you can say will convince me that this store is a good idea, Corey. The one thing I've always loved about this town is its unique character, and Main Street is a big part of that. Constructing a huge, window-less monstrosity of a store will do nothing but take away from the character and charm of Main Street."

"So, is that what your cleanup day is supposed to do? Help restore the character and charm of Main Street?"

"Don't call it *my* cleanup day. I just suggested it, but I can't take the lead on this."

"Why not?" Corey asked, mimicking her stance as he leaned against the back door and crossed his ankles. "You just said yesterday that you don't have anything to do over at Mrs. Eloise's. And I already offered to help out. Why don't we get together tomorrow afternoon after I'm done with baseball practice? We can go over ideas."

"I'm not sure that's a good idea. Spending time with you," she clarified when he looked confused.

"Come on, Mya. I'm not that bad."

"You, Corey Anderson, are the very definition of bad."

"Well, I am one of those Anderson boys," he said.

"It has nothing to do with you being one of those Anderson boys. You know that's not the kind of bad I'm talking about."

He flashed that smile again, and she went liquid. God, how could he still have this effect on her?

"Admit it," he said in a low, way-too-sexy-for-her-own-good voice. "You like being bad with me."

She swallowed deep. "Liked. Past tense," Mya said. "And, yes, I liked it way too much."

Looking over at him, she tilted her head to the side. There was a time when the man standing next to her could get her to do just about anything. He was just a boy back then, but he had consumed her every waking thought. Mya was sure he had no idea the power he wielded over her. She would have moved heaven and earth to please him.

A smile touching her lips, she shook her head. "You always were my favorite mistake."

He covered his chest as if she'd struck him. "Ouch. A mistake? That's harsh, Peaches."

Mya didn't bother to correct him. As frightening as it was to admit, she got a slight thrill at hearing the long-ago nickname roll so effortlessly off his tongue. Memories of other times he'd whispered that name in her ear sent tendrils of heat cascading along her skin.

It was a bad idea to allow those thoughts to invade her mind.

"I need to go," Mya said with an abrupt start. "Grandma is expecting a report on tonight's meeting."

She opened the car door, but Corey reached across the open space, bracing his hand on the doorjamb. "Are we meeting tomorrow?" he asked. "Just to discuss plans. I promise."

That word slapped her in the face. Sobering, Mya said, "From what I remember, your promises aren't always kept."

He dropped his hands, along with the smile that had been on his lips. "Mya," he said with a defeated sigh.

She didn't wait for the rest of his response as she ducked into the car. Slipping behind the wheel, she started the engine and pulled out of the parking lot.

Mya knocked gently on the door to her grandmother's hospital room, not wanting to disturb her if she was sleeping.

"Come in," Aunt Mo called.

She pushed the door open and laughed at the sight before her. A serious game of cards was in progress, and judging by the pile of cotton balls stacked on Grandma's side of the small tray table, she was whipping Aunt Mo's butt.

"All this place needs is dim lighting and a haze of hovering cigar smoke," Mya said.

"Just let me win this hand," Grandma

said. "Then you can fill me in on what happened tonight."

A minute later, Aunt Mo was pushing away from the bed and mumbling about cheaters. Mya took her spot, gathering the cotton balls and placing them in the plastic bin that was supposed to serve as a washtub.

"First things first," Mya said. "What did the doctors tell you today?"

"My sugar is under control," Grandma announced. "All four readings today were in the safe range, so it looks as if I'll be changing to this new insulin."

"And the anemia?"

"The doctor thinks it'll be okay if she adds more iron to her diet," Aunt Mo said from the recliner that had served as her bed for the past two nights. "They're discharging her tomorrow morning."

Mya's shoulders slumped with relief. "That's wonderful."

"I don't know about that," her grandmother said. "Are you going back to New York now that I'm on my way home?" The layer of guilt in those words was thicker than molasses.

"I don't think I'll be leaving that soon," Mya sighed. "Especially now that I'm the head of the Gauthier Civic Association's Cleanup Day."

A whoop of laughter came from Aunt Mo. "What did those women talk you into?"

Mya gave them the rundown on the night's meeting, with Grandma stopping her to interject comments. Her eyes beamed with pride when Mya told her about her suggestion to get the community involved in sprucing up Main Street, and how the entire group loved it.

"That is exactly what this town needs," Grandma said. She covered Mya's hand and gave it a gentle squeeze. "Thank you for agreeing to do this."

If her grandmother knew how close Mya had been to bolting from that classroom, she wouldn't be looking at her as if she were Mother Teresa reincarnated.

"It isn't that big of a deal," Mya said, smoothing the edges on the thin bedsheet before pushing up from the chair.

"Yes, it is," her grandmother said. "Main Street is the heart of this community. If those developers see how strong the support is for local business, then maybe we can get them to stop sniffing around."

Mya crossed her arms over her chest. "What do you have to say about your new best friend, Corey, being the new store's biggest cheerleader?"

Her grandmother shot her a frustrated

scowl. "I've tried to tell him better, but he's hardheaded."

"He says the developers plan to work with the local businesses."

That statement got her another disapproving glower. "They say that now, but I know how these big companies work. They'll drop their prices until no one else can compete with them, and after they've run all the other stores out of business, that's when they'll jack the prices up." Her grandmother wagged a finger at her. "You mark my words. If we let those developers set up shop here, it'll be the beginning of the end of this town as we know it."

Mya leaned over and kissed her grandmother's forehead. "You don't have to worry about that. Gauthier isn't going anywhere."

Mya was taken aback by the comfort that accompanied that thought. For someone who had spent most of her youth itching to flee this town, she couldn't deny the sense of security she'd derived in seeing that so much of Gauthier had remained the same. This town — these people — would always be a part of her.

Despite the disruption it would cause to her nicely structured life, Mya knew she wouldn't be buying a return ticket to New

York anytime soon. New York would always be there. She owed it to Gauthier to make sure the same could be said for her hometown.

CHAPTER 6

Corey gulped down half the cup of sweetened iced tea as he read over the expense reports from last season's games. The school board's financial director had warned him that Gauthier High's athletic department would probably face budget cuts. He was preparing himself for when *probably* became *definitely.*

"You look like someone just stole your bicycle."

Corey's head popped up. A grin tugged at the corner of his mouth as he watched Mya stroll toward the wooden picnic table he'd commandeered underneath the carport at Jessie's. She looked good enough to eat.

"Just work," he said, closing the manila folder and scooting over on the bench to make a spot for her. She walked over to the other side and sat across from him. That was probably for the best. For the past few days, he hadn't been thinking straight when it came to Mya.

"I can't believe this place hasn't been shut down yet," she remarked, her eyes roaming around the open-air carport that was attached to Jessie LeBlanc's woodframe house. "I'm no expert on Louisiana state law, but I believe it's illegal to run a restaurant out of your home's kitchen."

"And that's supposed to stop Jessie?" Corey laughed. "She caters the Policemen's Banquet every year."

"Gotta love small towns where things like proper licenses and permits don't matter."

"Can you smell that fried fish? Who cares whether or not she has a permit?" Corey rose from the picnic table and entered through the screen door that led to the back porch. Rapping lightly on the open kitchen door, he ordered two plates of fried catfish with a side of potato salad and two sweetened iced teas.

When he returned to the table, Mya was gazing toward the huge oak tree in Jessie's backyard, a wistful smile tilting her lips.

"I know why you're smiling," Corey said as he slid onto the bench.

She brought her gaze to him and quirked a brow.

He folded his arms on the table and leaned forward. Heavy on the husky, he murmured, "Junior year. Gauthier versus Slidell High School. I hit three home runs, and you rewarded me over by that oak tree."

Her smile broadened as she slid a heavy-lidded gaze back toward the tree. "Everyone was sitting here under the carport eating burgers. They never even realized we were gone."

"And we just slipped right back here after we were done," Corey said, his gut tightening at the memory.

"You talked me into doing the wildest things," Mya murmured.

"Nah-uh." Corey shook his head. "That time, you're the one who did the talking. I was sitting over there with the guys." He pointed to the spot where Jessie used to keep an ice chest filled with free sodas for the team. "You caught my attention and lured me over to that oak tree."

Her eyes widened and her grin turned into a full-on smile. "I remember now," she said.

"You seduced me, Mya Dubois. I was like an innocent little lamb being led to slaughter."

She barked out a laugh. "Don't even try it. Everything I knew about seduction, I learned from you."

Corey reached across the table and fingered her slim wrist. "I taught you well."

The pulse beneath her delicate skin escalated as his gaze silently, steadily bore into hers. As the heat of the shared memory burned hotter than the midday sun, Corey leaned forward, the impulse to taste her mouth overriding his senses.

The minute his lips met hers, he was catapulted back in time, to an era when his entire world revolved around getting to do this very thing as much as possible. He traced his tongue along Mya's lips, urging them to part. When they did, Corey dove into the moist warmth, probing, seeking, unearthing her unique flavor.

Angling his head, he deepened the kiss, reacquainting himself with a mouth he had not tasted in fifteen long years. She tasted just as he remembered — sweet with a hint of spice.

With a pained moan, Mya abruptly pulled away from him.

"Stop this, Corey," she said, her chest rising and falling with her deep breaths. "I'm not going there with you again, so just stop it."

Corey suppressed the curse on the tip of his tongue. She was resisting him. He refused to believe she was immune to these rekindled feelings.

He wouldn't call her on it . . . yet. But he

would prove that she was as affected by him as he was by her.

He flipped the pages of his notebook until he found a clean sheet. "Are we ready to get started?" he asked.

With a shaky hand — evidence that she had been affected by their kiss — Mya gestured to the folders sprawled out on the picnic table. "Did you have something else you needed to finish?" She pulled a pen and paper from the bag she'd brought with her.

"Not really," Corey said. "This paperwork isn't going anywhere. I'll get it done tomorrow."

She shot him a quizzical look. "I always wondered what coaches did during the day while their players are in class."

"This coach teaches economics and American history," Corey answered. He was pretty sure the shocked expression on her face should have offended him, but it was too funny for him to be upset.

He nodded. "Believe it or not, I'm good for something other than swinging a baseball bat and hot-wiring cars. Who would have thought, huh?"

That garnered him a chastising frown. "Stop that," she said. "You know I never thought you were only good for swinging a baseball bat."

"What about hot-wiring cars?"

"I'm being serious, Corey. I thought you dropped out of college to play in the major leagues?" she asked.

"I left after my junior year, but I continued to take classes during the off-season until I earned my degree."

"I had no idea." She fiddled with a couple of salt and pepper packets that had been left on the picnic table. "Do you miss it?" she asked after a few moments had passed.

"Baseball?" Corey shrugged. "Of course I do. Baseball was my life."

"I watched your games whenever I could," she said. "Both while you were in college and when you joined the Arizona Diamondbacks."

Corey fully owned the joy that single admission induced. He had always hoped she'd kept tabs on him once she left Gauthier, but he'd had too much pride to inquire from her grandmother whether Mya asked about him when she called home.

"Those were good times," he said. "But I'm enjoying coaching. When the doctors told me my shoulder injury was career-ending, I thought the game would be lost to me forever. It's pretty satisfying to be able to put my baseball knowledge to good use, you know?"

Why was he telling her all of this? She'd asked him to help come up with a plan for sprucing up Main Street, not recap his life story. Maybe if she didn't look so damn interested in what he was saying, he'd shut up.

Thankfully, Jessie's granddaughter appeared, balancing two plates of perfectly fried catfish and rounded scoops of potato salad along with two plastic cups of iced tea.

"So, what are your thoughts for this cleanup day?" Corey asked as he broke off a piece of fish, more than ready to shift the topic of conversation away from himself.

Mya stared at him for a moment longer, then mercifully flipped the cover open on her notepad. "I jotted down a few ideas. Most of the stores do a good job taking care of their own property, but the public areas could use some work. We don't have a huge budget to work with, but if we can get enough people to pitch in with the labor, we can use our dollars for other things.

"I'm going to try to solicit as many donations as possible. I talked to Campbell's Nursery over in Bogalusa, and the owner is willing to sell us seedlings and bulbs at cost. We're going to add shrubbery around the base of the lampposts and some more flowers to the landscaping in Heritage Park."

"You're really getting into this, aren't you?"

Mya shrugged. "Grandma and I were talking about it earlier today. She was so excited. I guess she's rubbing off on me."

As they feasted on fried catfish and diabetes-inducing sweet iced tea, they broke the cleaning tasks into categories and estimated how many people would be needed for each group in order to get the work done.

"You won't have a problem convincing your players to pitch in, will you?"

"Don't worry about the team," Corey said. "And I'm pretty sure you'll get people from the area churches to help out."

"You're right. No town rallies behind a cause quite like Gauthier. I still remember when that political group from up north tried to stop the living nativity from taking place in Heritage Park."

"People take their Christmas celebrations seriously around here."

Her eyes crinkled in amusement. "Speaking of celebrations, I need to head over to the library. I promised Grandma I would help write the town's history for the pamphlet she wants to put together for the anniversary celebration. Hey, you think Leroy

Gauthier would have some info? Maybe I should stop in at his law office."

"Leroy Gauthier is an appellate court judge in New Orleans. His son Matthew took over the family practice."

"Little Matt Gauthier?"

"He's not all that little. He was only a few years behind us," Corey said. "But it wouldn't hurt to ask. The town is named after their family, after all. Maybe he has some old stories passed down at reunions that the rest of us don't know about."

She pushed her empty plate to the side and flipped the cover on her notepad. The sight of her preparing to leave pinched his chest. "You're not going to have any of Jessie's bread pudding?" Corey asked, trying to think of any reason to get her to stay just a few minutes longer.

"It's bad enough I wolfed down that fried fish," she said. "I'll need to jog from here to Maplesville to work off this food."

Corey dragged his eyes in a deliberately slow perusal up and down Mya's incredibly toned body. At thirty-two she was in better shape than someone half her age.

"Your body is one thing you don't have to worry about," he said.

"Don't look at me like that, Corey."

"How am I looking at you?"

"Like you've decided I would be a better dessert than Jessie's bread pudding."

They were just words, but the image they brought to mind made him harder than forged steel. His tongue darted out of his mouth, and he licked his lips, remembering the taste a fifteen-year dearth could not obliterate.

"It's not even a question," he said. "Just let me know when you're ready to get on the menu."

He was well acquainted with that glazed look that came over her eyes. He had rendered her speechless with his lips and fingers and tongue enough times to know her body's every reaction.

Trying to start up anything with Mya was just asking for frustration and heartache. His rational side knew it as fact, but the part of him that burned like a bonfire for her was waging an all-out campaign to get into Mya Dubois's pants. It was as if the raging hormones of the guys on his baseball team had somehow rubbed off on him. He was a grown man. He shouldn't be sporting wood after a few minutes of light flirting and one kiss. But he'd be damned if he wasn't hard as a brick. Only Mya could have this effect on him.

"Thanks for the early dinner," she said.

"I'll let you know if I'm able to get anything from Matthew Gauthier."

Corey turned around on the bench and rested his elbows on the picnic table as he watched her march to her aunt's car. She was rattled, and he wasn't so sure it was a good thing. The last time he'd rattled Mya, she'd left town and stayed away for fifteen years.

Then again, it was pretty much a certainty that she would leave again in a matter of days. He'd better do as much rattling as he could while he still had the chance.

Mya stuffed the old book bag she'd found in the closet between the spare tire and the box of clothes marked Goodwill in Maureen's trunk. She went back into the house and grabbed a bottled water from the fridge before stopping in the living room where her grandmother lounged in her grandfather's soft leather recliner.

"You'll be okay?" Mya asked, bending over and placing a kiss on her forehead.

"Of course," she said. "It's not as if your aunt will let me do anything."

"Do you know what 'take it easy' means?" Maureen called from the laundry room. "I can bring you back to the hospital so the doctor can explain it again."

Her grandmother looked up at Mya and rolled her eyes. Then she turned her attention back to the television. "That Paula Deen knows she likes herself some butter. Look at that."

"Please don't have a twelve-thousand-calorie pound cake baking when I get back," Mya pleaded. She was sure she'd gained five pounds in the week she'd been in Gauthier.

"Mama knows better than to try baking pound cake," Maureen yelled.

"You sure you don't need company on your trip to Baton Rouge?" her grandmother drawled.

"No. I still remember how to get to Baton Rouge, and I borrowed Phylicia's navigation system to guide me to the state library."

"Thank you again for doing this, baby," her grandmother said. "I know you hadn't planned on any of this when you came home."

"I told you it's not a problem," Mya assured her. "I'm just hoping I have better luck at the state library. There has to be more on this town's history than what I could find in the library here, and Matthew Gauthier was no help at all."

"He's a busy lawyer, even in this small town," Grandma said.

"I'll probably be gone most of the day

since just the drive will take three hours round trip. Aunt Mo?" Mya called. "You sure you're okay with me taking your car?"

Maureen came into the room, wiping her hands on a dish towel that she then tossed onto her shoulder. "Little girl, how many times do I have to tell you to take the dang car?"

Mya grinned. "Thank you. And unlike I used to do in high school, I'll be sure to bring it back with a full tank."

"You'd better," Maureen warned.

Mya gave them both parting kisses before heading out of the house. Her steps slowed as Corcy's Escalade pulled up. He climbed out of the SUV, sunglasses covering his eyes. His freshly pressed shorts and polo shirt were definitely not for cutting grass.

Still, Mya said, "You're a week early, aren't you? I thought you cut Grandma's grass every *other* Saturday?"

"I'm not here to do yard work," he said. "I'm coming with you to the library in Baton Rouge."

"Excuse me?"

He shot her a grin as he walked over to Maureen's car, opened the passenger door and got in.

Mya looked up to the sky as if it would provide answers, then went over to the car and leaned into the open driver's-side window. "How did you even know I was going to the state library, and why would you think I need you to tag along?"

"Because Mrs. Eloise mentioned it when I called to see how she was doing yesterday, and because you like my company."

He flashed a set of perfectly white teeth, and Mya was tempted to run into the house and grab another one or two or *ten* bottles of water. Corey Anderson was temptation incarnate, and with all the extra time she had on her hands, spending any of it with him was a green light for trouble.

"Do you expect me to believe you have nothing better to do than to ride all the way to Baton Rouge to search through dusty library books?"

"Believe it," he said. "Come on, Mya. Even though I still think this new store is the best thing for Gauthier, I told you I would help with the work you're doing for the civic association. This is me helping." He gestured with his head. "You'd better get in the car. It's a long drive to Baton Rouge."

The prospect of being confined to a car with him for several hours set off a string of alarm bells in her head. Their bodies went with backseats the way peanut butter went with jelly.

Sensing his resolve, she gave up her futile effort to get rid of him and slid behind the wheel.

"And who says I like your company?" she grumbled as she jabbed the key into the ignition and started the car.

Corey's head tilted back with his deep, rich laugh.

Nearly an hour into their drive on Interstate 12, Mya was once again struck by the ease with which she found herself conversing with Corey. In a way, it felt as if the tension and distance of their fifteen-year estrangement had never existed. Mya was surprised to learn that he'd followed her career after her Tony nomination had put her on the proverbial map for costume design.

"Do you think you're going to stick to Broadway, or have you considered maybe going to Hollywood and working in the movies?" he asked.

"The thought never crossed my mind," Mya admitted. "I love New York too much."

Corey huffed out a genuine laugh. "I never understood how a girl who grew up in a small town like Gauthier could feel comfortable in the big city. It seems so impersonal."

"But it's not," Mya said. "That's one of

the biggest misconceptions people have about New York. It's not impersonal at all. It's made up of dozens of small neighborhoods where people look out for each other. That's what I love about it. There's this feeling of community."

"You had that here," Corey stated.

Mya took her eyes off the road for a moment to glance at him. The set of his jaw was as rigid as stone.

"Why did you really leave?" The question held no accusation, just honest curiosity. "Maybe I shouldn't ask that. I already know why you left."

Her heart stopped; for a full three seconds it congealed with fear that he had somehow found out about the baby she'd miscarried. Her heartbeats resumed only after Corey continued, "I know I hurt you when I slept with Tamika Hillard on graduation night. I've never forgiven myself for that. You do know it was only that one time, right?"

She nodded, and her throat pinched with guilt as she remembered the knock-down, drag-out argument they'd had when she caught him with her rival on the cheerleading squad. She had let him believe that his infidelity was the reason she was breaking up with him and leaving Gauthier, even though Mya had already made the decision to leave the night she'd lain in a hospital bed after losing his baby. Two weeks prior to graduation.

"I've forgiven you," she said.

"You have?"

"It was a long time ago, Corey. What good does it do anyone to hold on to the anger and resentment?"

"But I hurt you so badly that night."

"You did," she said in a small voice. "And it made me want to leave Gauthier even more, but it wasn't the only reason I left."

"I know it's not the *only* reason you left," he said. "You always talked about getting out of Gauthier and making a life for yourself. What I really want to know is why didn't you come back? What made you stay away for all those years? You had to know it was hurting your grandparents."

Mya swallowed the rock-hard lump that formed in her throat. She'd asked herself that same question so many times it had been permanently etched into her soul. She had tried to come back over the years, had made it all the way to the airline gate once. But something had always held her back.

Fear.

It was fear that had made her gut clench whenever she thought of coming back here. Fear of being sucked into the teenage

125

pregnancy trap that had snared girls like Shelly. Fear that she would get stuck in this small town and never experience anything outside of it. She had been so, *so* afraid. And those fears had all combined to create an invisible barrier that had, until one week ago, blocked her return to Gauthier.

But she couldn't tell that to Corey. He would never understand that way of thinking. Even after people here shunned him, he'd still returned. He would never understand how something as intangible as fear could keep her away.

"Time just got away from me," Mya said instead. "One year turned into another and then another. And, just like that, fifteen had gone by." She tightened her grip on the steering wheel. "I still saw my grandparents, though. I flew them up to New York at least once a year, sometimes more."

"It's not the same as you being here," he said.

"Does it count that I'm here now?" Mya asked, glancing over at Corey.

One edge of his mouth lifted in a brief smile, and he said, "Yeah. It does."

A half hour later they pulled into a parking spot adjacent to the Louisiana State Library. She popped the trunk before getting out and grabbing her backpack.

"That brings back memories," Corey commented, eyeing the bag.

Mya held up the backpack and grinned. "I became a pro at fitting an extra set of clothes in with all of my school books," she said. "Two, depending on if there was more than one party on a Friday night."

"I really was a bad influence, wasn't I?" His smirk was pure sin.

"Oh, yeah." Mya nodded. She regarded him with subtle amusement. "But it was the best kind of bad."

His grin deepened with shared remembrance, and Mya had to mentally stave off images of all the deliciously bad things Corey used to do to her. Even at seventeen he'd had skills to rival a man twice his age and with double the experience.

As they climbed the steps of the four-story, glass-fronted building, his arm brushed against hers, setting her already heated skin to danger-zone temperatures. Mya wasn't sure how much longer she could fight this lust without going insane.

He opened the door and motioned for her to go ahead of him.

"I checked out the website, and from what I gathered the best place to start looking would be the Louisiana Collection," Mya told him.

She headed straight for the information desk and was pointed in the direction of the room that housed books and documents pertaining to Louisiana history and culture. It was practically deserted, with only one other person sitting at a square table. Mya went for the farthest table on the opposite end of the room.

"Where should we start?" Corey asked in the hushed tone one's voice automatically assumed when in a library.

She pulled the notepad from her backpack and flipped it open. "I wrote down the titles of a few books that may have some information. I also want to look through the newspapers. The library has copies of the *Gauthier Courier* and *Maplesville Gazette* on microfiche."

Mya enlisted the help of a librarian to set her up at a microfiche machine while Corey went in search of books. After a quick tutorial in how to use the machine, Mya turned the knob on the first film and her heart immediately sunk.

"Oh, crap." The paper was in French, which made sense since that was the predominant language in the area back then. "Well, this is going to be harder than I thought," she murmured.

She returned to the information desk,

hoping there was some sort of electronic translator she could borrow, but the desk was unoccupied. Figuring the librarian's absence was nothing more than a short bathroom break, she went over to the stacks to see if Corey had managed to find one of the titles on her list. She found him sand-wiched between the walls of books, his head bent over a thick tome. He looked up at her and Mya's breath caught.

He wore a pair of thin, wire-rimmed glasses. They were, without a doubt, the sexiest set of spectacles to ever grace a man's face.

"Any luck with the newspaper?" he asked, completely unaware that just the sight of him in those unassuming glasses had her blood racing like a marathoner's.

Mya coughed in an attempt to clear the lust from her throat. "It's in French," she said.

"Makes sense," he said. "There may be an English version. Some of the papers had started printing in both."

She was about to ask how he knew that, then remembered that he taught American history. Corey Anderson, heart-stoppingly handsome, cocksure, bad-ass baseball star was now a high school history teacher. Mya still had a hard time correlating the two.

"I'll ask the librarian," she said. "Have you found anything?"

He shrugged a well-muscled shoulder. "Just your typical rundown of how so many of the towns were formed back then," Corey continued. "Slavery is abolished. The slaves are given some land to start their new lives. And, abracadabra, a new town is born."

"I figured as much," she said. "But as long as I find *something* to put in Grandma's pamphlet, she'll be happy." She gazed at the stern slant of his jaw as he concentrated on what he was reading. It was strong, but she knew from experience that his skin was soft as butter. "I guess I'll check to see if the librarian is back at her desk."

"Okay," Corey said, not looking up from the book.

Mya stared at him for several moments, captivated by the way his light blue polo shirt stretched across his chest, and how the fluorescent lights illuminated his close-cut, naturally wavy hair. He truly was a beautiful specimen.

He looked up from the book and cocked an inquiring brow. "Need something else?"

"No," Mya said with a vigorous shake of her head. "I'm . . . uh . . . going to the . . . over there." She pointed toward the microfiche room.

The knowing grin that crinkled the corners of Corey's eyes sent a shower of embarrassment over her. She was a grown, sophisticated, urban woman, yet one smile from him could reduce her to acting like the small-town country girl who had worshipped him all those years ago.

Mya marched over to the librarian's desk and — *thank you, God!* — found the woman behind her computer. The librarian helped her to find English versions of the *Maplesville Gazette* and several other papers from surrounding towns. Before long, Mya was completely engrossed. She was startled when she glanced down at her cell phone and realized that more than an hour had passed.

She heard footsteps approach and Corey's gently whispered, "Knock, knock," just over her shoulder. Mya turned and was once again caught off guard by how sexy he looked in those glasses.

"I think I found something," he said, excitement lighting up his eyes. He rolled a chair from a nearby microfiche station and sat at an angle to her. Pointing to a spot on the page, he said, "According to the historian who wrote this book, Micah Gauthier and his wife, Nicollette, were both arrested for harboring slaves in their home during the time of the Underground Railroad, and they were known to sympathize with the abolitionist movement." He looked up at her. "Their home was in the building that now houses Matthew Gauthier's law practice."

It took Mya a moment to comprehend the enormity of his words.

"Oh, my God," she whispered. "Are you telling me that Gauthier was a stop on the Underground Railroad? Corey, this is huge. I mean this is really, *really* huge."

"I'm a history teacher, remember? I know how huge this is. It's more than just huge, Mya. It's historic. This changes everything."

Mya pushed back from behind the microfiche station and started pacing, trying to piece together the thoughts that crowded her brain. "Okay, okay. Let's calm down," she said. "First things first. We need to contact the state's historical society."

"No, the first thing we need to do is get back to those books and find out more about what went down back then. We're going to need documented evidence before we go to the historical society."

"You're right," she said. He just looked at her with a look that said, *well, duh! History teacher here.*

"We also need to find out what other

132

historical sites there are in Gauthier," Corey continued. "I'll bet Matthew Gauthier's law practice isn't the only place with some historical significance."

Mya pointed to the archives room. "You get back to the books. I'll use one of the computers on the main floor to see if I can find what kind of documentation is needed for the historical society and the state's tourism board. There should be something on their websites."

"The tourism board?"

"Of course," Mya said. She realized she hadn't taken the time to share the ideas that had bombarded her brain. "Corey, don't you see what this means for Gauthier? People travel to New Orleans for three things: food, music and the history. Gauthier is less than an hour's drive away." She paused for a moment, remembering. "Do those tour buses still go out to that plantation home in Maplesville?"

"Every Tuesday," Corey said, understanding flourishing in his gray-brown eyes.

Mya's mouth curved in a conspiratorial grin. "They're about to add an extra stop to their tour." She leaned over to peer at the pages of the book, but could make nothing out under the dimmed lights of the microfiche room. "Does it say anything else that the people back home should know?"

When Corey didn't continue, Mya looked up to find him staring at her. "What?" she asked at his curious expression.

"You just called it 'home.' I like that you still think of it that way," Corey said. "There's a lot to love about Gauthier."

Like the fact that he was there, Mya thought. His presence was like a beacon, drawing her into the clutches of a life she'd abdicated so long ago.

It was also what made her want to get out of Dodge as soon as possible.

Just as he'd been all those years ago, Corey was a threat to the freedom and independence she'd claimed for herself. He induced dangerous thoughts, elicited images of an era when she would have contemplated remaining in Gauthier just to be with him. She'd left that girl — that space in time — behind.

She would not give up the life she'd built for herself for anyone, not even Corey Anderson.

Corey stood in the middle of the dark microfiche room watching Mya as she trekked a five-foot trough into the carpet. She continued to rattle off ideas about how to incorporate their discovery into the town's anniversary celebration. The more excited she became, the faster she talked. She used to do the same thing back when they were in school together.

"You know, there are companies that specialize in tours specific to African-American history in the South. They would jump on this. We can put together a walking tour of the town. Take them along Main Street, through Heritage Park, and then for lunch at Emile's. It could be a package deal."

It had been less than ten minutes since they had discovered there was anything worth seeing in Gauthier and she already had tour groups eating crab bisque at Emile's. They first had to go through the rigors of getting the site in Gauthier acknowledged by the state's historical society, which he was sure was no easy feat. But Corey wouldn't put a damper on her enthusiasm. He was enjoying seeing Mya once again excited about their hometown.

She wasn't the only one who was excited. The history buff in him was still reeling from this discovery.

Just yesterday Corey had been 100 percent on board with the potential construction of a national retail chain on Main Street, but this new discovery changed everything. If it turned out that Gauthier had indeed been a stop on the Underground Railroad, history buffs like himself would flock here. And making sure the downtown area maintained the essence of an authentic Main Street U.S.A. would be critical to the town's appeal as a tourist destination. A big-box retail store no longer fit into the equation.

As stoked as Corey was about their finding, he was just as excited that he had been part of the team who'd discovered it. It was that part of him that was still aching to show the people in Gauthier that he'd changed from being the bad boy that used to wreak havoc with his brothers.

"We're going to need to get in touch with the rest of the civic association," Mya said. "This changes the focus of the celebration. We need to make this about playing up the history of Gauthier."

"Don't worry about that now," Corey said. He reached out and captured her arm, stalling her back-and-forth march.

She looked down at where he held her arm, then trailed her gaze to his face.

"You're going to wear a hole in the carpet," Corey told her.

Mya blew out a weary breath. "I'm sorry. I can't control myself when I'm excited."

"Just calm down," Corey said, bringing

his other hand up to cover her arm. He rubbed her soft skin. "Let's take a minute to just enjoy what we've discovered, then we can figure out where to go from here. Sound good?"

She sucked in another deep breath and nodded, but the calm didn't last long. Excitement had her eyes lighting up like fireworks. "This is really cool, isn't it? I mean, you being a history teacher and all, you should know."

"It's very cool," he assured her, squeezing her upper arm. "If this discovery pans out, this may turn out to be the biggest thing to happen to Gauthier in over a century."

A comfortable stretch of time passed as they continued to stare into each other's eyes. Mya's eyes took on a smoky quality as she gazed up at him.

"We always did make a good team," she said, her voice husky.

"Always," he agreed. He lowered his head and brushed his lips against hers.

"Corey," she whispered against his lips. But it was spoken too softly to be a protest. He took it as encouragement.

Corey bathed her lips with his tongue, back and forth, molding his mouth to hers, urging her to open for him. With excruciating sweetness her resistance relented, making way for his tongue to sweep in. He slipped an arm around her waist and settled his hand at the small of her back.

"God, you taste good," he whispered against her lips.

The soft moan that rumbled deep in her throat traveled along his skin like a caress. She brought her hand up to the back of his head and held him in place.

Corey's body ignited with sparks of desire. They ricocheted against the walls of his chest, imprisoning his breath. He clamped his palms on Mya's firm backside and pulled her flush against him, nearly dying at how perfectly she fit into the cove of his body. She was soft and warm and woman, smelling like spring, tasting like heaven.

Just as he remembered.

Corey devoured her, stroking the inside of her mouth as he recalled those long-ago moments they'd shared. The times she'd given herself fully to him, allowing him the pleasure of her sweet mouth and that succulent body that still turned him on like no other woman ever could.

He trailed his tongue down her neck and nestled his face against her skin, breathing in the arousing scent that was all Mya.

"Damn, I want you," he groaned against her neck.

She moaned, but then pulled back. "Wait. No," she said, bringing both hands up and pushing against his chest.

He went for her mouth again, but she pressed her fingers against his lips. "No." She shook her head. "We can't do this."

Corey's shoulders sunk in defeat. "Why not?"

"Because," she said with finality.

Based on her tone, Corey knew from experience that that was all the answer he would get. Mya disengaged from his hold and took several steps back.

He dropped his head back and grimaced at the ceiling. "It's just a kiss, Mya. Don't make such a big deal out of it."

"It was never just a kiss with you," she said. "Just a kiss always led to so much more."

Corey cocked his head to the side as he stared at her in the dim light of the room. "Would that really be so bad?" he asked. "We're not seventeen anymore, Mya. We're two intelligent, single, consenting adults."

She crossed her arms over her chest and jutted out her chin. "What makes you think I'm single?"

The question hit his chest with the force of a hundred-mile-per-hour fastball.

As ridiculous as it was to think she'd gone

fifteen years without ever being with someone else, Corey could never stomach the thought of Mya with another man. But there was no way she was seeing anyone right now. He was certain of it. Even if she'd dated a hundred men over the years, she wouldn't have let him get so close if she were in a relationship.

"You never would have let me kiss you if you were attached," he told her. "Don't try to play me, Mya Dubois. I know you better than just about anybody, even after all these years."

"It doesn't matter," she said after a pause. "This is still a bad idea. I'm only here for a few weeks at the most."

"So why can't we enjoy those few weeks? It's better than nothing."

Corey closed the gap between them and trailed a finger down her forearm, feeling her flesh pebble with tiny goose bumps. He loved that his touch could still elicit such a reaction from her.

"Tell me you haven't been thinking about how we were together. We were damn good, Mya. You can't deny that."

She rolled her shoulder slowly, pulling away from his touch.

"And you can't deny that it ended badly, with you breaking my heart."

"It was one drunken mistake, and I was seventeen years old. It was the one and only time I ever cheated on you. That I've ever cheated in my entire life."

"Once was enough," she retorted. "Do you know how long it took me to get over you?"

"Not as long as it took me," Corey said, moving in closer. "Because I'm still not over you."

Mya's eyelids slid shut. "Don't say that," she pleaded with a weary sigh.

"It's true, Mya. You're not the kind of woman a man easily gets over." Corey took the chance of reaching for her hand again. He took both between his palms and gave them a gentle squeeze. "I'm sorry for the way I hurt you that night. It's one of my biggest regrets." Corey trailed a finger along her soft cheek. "But now that we have a second chance, why can't we see where this leads?"

Her entire body shuddered with the deep breath she exhaled. She watched him intently. "My good sense tells me this is a mistake," she said.

"Tell your good sense to mind its own business," Corey teased.

He could sense the war raging inside of her as her mind battled against her body's response to him. He wanted her body to win the war. He could work on her mind later.

"C'mon, Mya. Aren't you the least bit curious to see what I've learned in fifteen years?"

She released a breathless laugh. "As I recall, there wasn't much you *didn't* know fifteen years ago."

"Sweetheart, you have no idea." He caught her wrist and pulled her against him. Burying his head in the crook of her neck, Corey nipped at her delicate skin. "What do you say, Peaches?"

With a moan she tilted her head to the side and gave him full access to her neck. Her hand snaking up the back of his head, she sighed and said, "I guess some mistakes are too good not to make again."

CHAPTER 7

Mya rested her head against the headrest, trying her hardest to continue the relaxed facade she'd maintained since losing her mind and allowing Corey to kiss her again back at the library. She closed her eyes, allowing the gentle sway of the car to lull her brain into believing everything was okay. But everything was *so* not okay.

Kissing Corey was like eating an entire chocolate cake in one sitting. She knew it was a bad idea, but it felt too good in the moment to stop.

And his suggestion to pick up where they had left off fifteen years ago?

Madness. Complete and utter madness.

And so much more dangerous than chocolate cake. She could take care of the damage of cake with a couple of workouts. Recovering from the destruction Corey could do to her heart would take a hell of a lot more.

"Are you sleeping or just resting your eyes?" came Corey's soft voice. Mya lolled her head to the side and lifted her eyelids. He glanced from the road to her. "I didn't mean to wake you."

"You didn't," Mya assured him, straightening in the seat. "Did you need something?"

"We need to call an emergency meeting with the civic association, or at the very least with the members of the revitalization committee. We need to let them know what we've found. You think Mrs. Eloise would allow us to hold it at her house?"

"She would raise hell if we tried to hold it anywhere else."

The corner of his eye crinkled behind his dark sunshades. He steered one-handed while he pulled his cell from his pocket and tossed it to her. "Find Mrs. Claudette's number in my phone address book and give her a call. She'll make sure everyone is there. Just tell them we found something really big."

Mya made the call. As she waited for Claudette to pick up, she motioned toward the filling station a few yards ahead. "I promised Aunt Mo I'd top off her tank," she said.

Corey nodded and clicked on the signal

light, pulling up to a pump. Mya grabbed her purse and pulled out two twenties, but he waved her off. Before she could utter a protest, Claudette answered the phone.

"Hello, Claudette. It's Mya Dubois."

She explained that she and Corey had gone to the state library to research Gauthier's history and had uncovered a significant finding that the rest of the civic association needed to know about. When Claudette tried to get more details, Mya cut her off, telling her to just do her best to be at her grandmother's house at seven-thirty and to get as many members of the association there as well.

She then jotted down a list of refreshments Claudette advised her to pick up from the grocery store, because, apparently, if the association met, food must be involved. Mya made a quick call to her grandmother's to make sure it was okay that she'd just invited a houseful of people over. Mya briefly relayed the day's findings to Aunt Mo, but asked her not to say anything to her grandmother. She wanted to see Grandma's face when she learned of what Mya and Corey had unearthed about Gauthier's history.

When she was done with the calls she closed Corey's phone and glanced toward the convenience store. Mya did a double take as she watched Corey drag a teenager out of the store by his arm. She jumped out of the car and ran toward them.

"What's going on?" she barked.

"Nothing," Corey called over his shoulder. He got up in the boy's face. "Get your ass home now. I swear, Andre, I'd better not catch you doing something this stupid again."

Without saying a word, the boy took off and jumped into a late-model car with shiny rims on the tires.

"What was that about?" Mya asked.

His hands clenched into fists at his sides. "You remember Brandy Thomas?" he asked.

"Of course. She was on the cheerleading squad with me. Until she got pregnant junior year and dropped out of school."

He nodded toward the car that spewed loose gravel as it left the convenience store parking lot. "That's her son, Andre."

"Wow. Really?" She stared at the car. "I guess he would be that old, wouldn't he?"

"He's the best player on my team. Has scouts calling from Division One colleges around the country, all offering him scholarships. Yet I catch him trying to stuff two cans of beer under his shirt." Corey shook his head and started for the car. "I'm trying my hardest with this kid. He has so much damn potential, but he's throwing it all away."

Walking alongside him, Mya asked, "What does Brandy have to say about that?"

Corey got behind the wheel and started the car, but left it idling. "Brandy is serving twenty years at the women's correctional facility in St. Gabriel."

Mya gasped. "Oh, my God. For what?"

"Selling drugs, I think." He shrugged. "I never did get the whole story. Her younger sister, Kendra, is supposedly raising Andre, but every time I try to talk to her she —" He hesitated. "She changes the subject," Corey finished.

"Ah, yes. I remember Kendra in high school. She didn't really try to hide her feelings for you," Mya said.

Corey expelled a sigh. "She needs to focus more on Andre. I swear, he reminds me so much of myself at that age."

"Well, you didn't turn out so bad."

"Not for lack of trying," he said. "You remember the trouble me and my brothers got into after my dad had his first heart attack and could no longer handle us. But I was lucky. I had someone like Coach Edwards to step in and steer me on the right path. If he hadn't convinced that judge to let me off with a warning after I got arrested for stealing Donaldson's car all those years ago, who knows where I'd be?"

Corey slammed a fist against the steering wheel. "I'm trying to do for Andre what Coach Edwards did for me, but Andre is so damn hardheaded."

"So were you," Mya reminded him. "But Coach Edwards was even more hardheaded. He eventually got through to you. You'll get there with Andre."

"I don't know." Corey shook his head. "Andre's got a cousin, T.J., who is just plain no good. He reminds me of Shawn and Stefan."

At a loss for how to help him, Mya reached over and patted his thigh. "It'll be okay," she softly encouraged.

Corey looked down at her hand. "You're asking for trouble if you keep your hand there," he warned.

She jerked her hand away, mentally chastising herself. "Sorry."

He reached over and captured her hand, placing a delicate kiss to the inside of her palm. "I didn't say I had a problem with that kind of trouble, just wanted you to know what you were getting yourself into."

He leaned toward her and seized her lips in a slow, deliberate kiss. Mya tried to form a protest, but it felt too right to have his lips pressed against hers, his tongue delving into her mouth.

An hour later, Mya was perched on the arm of the sofa in her grandmother's living room, nibbling on potato chips and grinning as the five women who made up the civic association's revitalization committee gazed upon Corey with rapturous stares as he gave them an account of their findings.

"Mya and I have already gathered the information we need for contacting the local parish historical society. They have to check out the property first, then if they deem it a viable candidate, we go to the Louisiana Department of Historical Preservation."

"We're also going to work together to develop a package for the state tourism board," Mya added.

"I don't understand why nobody knew about this," Claudette said. "Most of us have lived here our entire lives."

Corey shrugged. "Not every bit of history makes it into the history books. Sometimes you have to dig. It's a good thing Mya decided to go the extra mile and dig a little deeper into Gauthier's history." The smile he slid her way warmed her cheeks and caused Mya to squirm on the edge of the sofa.

"So what do we do with this?" Clementine Washington asked.

Corey motioned for Mya to take center stage. She handed her plate of chips to Aunt Mo and dusted her fingers on the back of her pants as she stood before the ladies.

"We think that this is the kind of news that can completely change Gauthier."

"We don't want to change Gauthier," Margery piped in. "We like this town just fine."

"No, no," Mya said. "I didn't mean changing the town, but changing the way people *see* it. If it turns out that the Gauthier Law Firm was actually a part of the Underground Railroad and the historical society gives distinction to the town, we can make Gauthier a tourist destination. Schools would take field trips here. We can market it as a day trip for history buffs visiting New Orleans. And the shops on Main Street and the rest of the town's economy would benefit. You wouldn't change anything about Gauthier. In fact, you would make the town more like it used to be."

"And we think the 175th-year celebration is the perfect platform to kick this off," Corey said.

"What about that new store?" Barbara Cannon looked pointedly at Corey. "Are you still planning to become an investor?"

"No," Corey quickly said. "After what we uncovered today, I think we should keep the landscape of Main Street as close to its original form as possible. Adding a national chain store would take away from that."

"That's what we tried to tell you," Claudette said.

With a conciliatory grin, Corey put his hands up. "Yes, you all did. You win."

"Actually, Gauthier wins," Mya interjected.

Corey's eyes connected with hers and they shared a soft, private smile.

Or, maybe it wasn't so private. When Mya finally managed to tear her eyes from his, she noticed the sly smirks and knowing looks around the room. Aunt Maureen's brows arched in amused inquiry.

Mya cleared her throat, and hoped to God the blush warming her face wasn't evident.

"As I was saying," she began, "this link between Gauthier and the Underground Railroad truly is a game-changer. If we can get the people in town to rally behind this cleanup day, we can present Gauthier's best face to the preservation society."

"Are you planning to stay and see this

through?" her grandmother asked.

Mya looked over at her, then at the other faces that stared back at her.

"That's a good question," Corey said. "Are you?"

She couldn't feel more in the spotlight if one were shining down on her head. Mya looked from her grandmother to Corey to Aunt Mo, who was sitting on the sofa with a challenging smirk on her lips.

The walls closed in just a bit more, but Mya reminded herself that she always had a way out. All it would take was a quick call to an airline. The celebration was in three weeks. Twenty-one days. She could stick it out for twenty-one days.

"I'm in," she said.

But in twenty-one days, she would pack her bag and head back to New York.

Corey pulled his Escalade into a slanted slot on Main Street, a few yards away from the front door of Matthew Gauthier's law office. He'd had to cancel practice this afternoon while landscapers resodded the north end of the baseball field, but he wasn't complaining. When Mya called to ask if he was up to poking around the building that housed Gauthier Law Firm, he'd left the equipment room and headed straight here.

152

He spotted Maureen Dubois's dark blue sedan parked a few spaces down and couldn't hold back his grin. He'd been smiling like a damn fool ever since Mya announced to the entire revitalization committee that she would remain in Gauthier until the celebration.

No, that was a lie. He'd been smiling inside ever since he'd taken her into his arms and kissed them both breathless in the state library.

God, her mouth was sweet. Like a ripe, juicy peach on a hot summer day. It's how she'd earned her nickname. Now that he'd tasted her again, Corey didn't know how he was going to work alongside her and not seek out those decadent lips every five minutes.

He stepped inside the law office and found Mya engaged in an animated conversation with the receptionist. They both turned when he came upon them.

"Corey, did you know Carmen and Scotty Mitchell were married?" Mya asked, pointing to their former classmate Carmen Manheim, now Mitchell. Corey couldn't remember for certain, but he was sure Carmen had been voted most likely to get arrested . . . and throw a party in jail. The Manheim house had been known for its wild parties.

Corey nodded. "Their daughter, Malika, is in my ninth-grade American history class."

"And she hates it," Carmen laughed. "It's no reflection on you," she told Corey. "She hates all of her classes. All she wants to do is hang out with her friends. My mama warned me that I'd have a child who gave me as much problems as I gave her."

"She's a good student," Corey said. "If only she would shut up for more than a minute."

"Yep, just like her mom." Mya laughed.

Carmen treated her to an obscene hand gesture, and they both cracked up.

Corey nodded toward the closed door with a brass nameplate with *Matthew Gauthier, Esq.* engraved on it. "He knows we're coming, right?"

"He's on a call right now, but it should be finishing up in a few minutes. This is all so exciting." Carmen beamed. "Who knew this old building had so much history?"

"It's fascinating," Mya interjected, her enthusiasm coming through her voice. "I was up all night reading about the original owners, Micah and Nicollette Gauthier. They endangered their family for years by hiding runaway slaves here. I can't imagine."

"I wonder if Matthew knows this."

154

As if his receptionist had called him forth, the door opened and Matthew Gauthier, dressed in shirtsleeves and a tie, walked out carrying a briefcase. He greeted Mya with a kiss on her cheek and clasped Corey's palm in a firm shake.

"I hear we're sitting on some history in my grandfather's old office," he said.

"You're okay with us checking this place out, right?" Corey asked.

Matthew shrugged. "Not sure what you're looking for, but knock yourselves out."

"We heard that many of the stops on the Underground Railroad had secret hideaways where they stored the slaves," Mya said. "We were hoping you had run across some little nook, but since you said you hadn't, we just want to poke around a little."

Matthew swept his arm out in a welcoming gesture. "Have at it." He turned to Carmen. "I'm meeting Mr. Sellers at Emile's. I should be back before you close up at five, but if not, just leave the door unlocked."

"Unbelievable," Mya said. They all turned to her. "That you would just leave your office unlocked, even for a minute," she elaborated.

"One of the advantages of small-town life," Corey teased.

Carmen hung a Be Right Back sign on a

peg on the wall above her desk and took them on a tour of the building. They looked around Matthew's office, with its view of the wooden waterwheel in Heritage Park, then in the conference room and two smaller, unoccupied offices.

"The back room is mainly storage. Nothing confidential — those are locked away upstairs. Mr. Gauthier — Leroy — just hated to throw anything away," Carmen said as she led them into a cavernous room packed with neatly stacked banker boxes.

"Does Matthew realize the historical society may have to move all of these out of the way while they inspect the building?" Corey asked.

She waved him off. "Matthew won't care. He's so much more laid-back than his dad."

"Well, I don't want to disrupt all of this," Mya said.

"Just give me a heads-up when you hear back from the folks who will be inspecting," Carmen said.

Mya and Corey left the law practice and headed west on Main.

"What happened to Armant's Antiques Shop?" Mya asked, pointing to the only abandoned building on Main Street.

"It was closed before I moved back. From what I heard, after Mr. and Mrs. Armant both died, their son Elvin had a big garage sale where he sold everything for a dollar each."

"Yeah, from what I remember of Elvin, I can't really see him selling antiques," Mya said. "It's sad, though. I used to love looking around their shop. There was this gorgeous necklace."

"The one with the blue-and-green stones," Corey said.

She turned to him, her eyes widened in amazement. "You remember that sapphire-and-emerald necklace?"

"How many times did you drag me in there to look at it?" he asked.

A sheepish grin curled up the edges of her lips. It took everything within him not to lean over and kiss that smile. "Probably dozens," she said. "It was just so beautiful. Like something that would belong to the queen of England. God, I hope Elvin did not sell that necklace for a dollar. I would hunt him down and kill him."

"I'm sure he got top dollar for it," Corey laughed.

They reached the vine-covered arch that marked the entrance to Heritage Park. The square divided Main Street's east and west sections. Back when he was growing up, this park was where most families spent their

Saturday afternoons. The smell of charcoal saturated the air, and sounds of children playing on the swings and merry-go-round could be heard blocks away.

"I always loved this park," Corey commented.

"I know." Mya sighed. She stood just inside the entrance and panned the length of the park from east to west. "Does the waterwheel still work?"

"I think it does," Corey said. "They stopped running it because of utility costs. I don't think they turn on the lights over the arbor at night either," he said.

She looked up at him with sad eyes. "But it's so pretty when it's all lit up."

"Maybe after the cleanup day we can convince the parish council to light up the arbor again," he said.

"Speaking of the cleanup day, you wouldn't believe how many people have been calling the house to volunteer. I think the turnout is going to be better than anyone expected."

"You'd better watch it. It almost sounds as if you care what happens to this place." The hurt in her eyes made Corey regret he'd spoken. "I'm sorry," he offered.

"You make me sound heartless," she murmured. She wrapped her arms around her upper body as they walked over to the waterwheel. "I never said I didn't care about Gauthier. I just . . . wanted out."

He leaned a hip against the wooden railing of the log fence surrounding the waterwheel.

"Why?" Corey asked. "I never understood that about you. You hated your mother because she hightailed it out of Gauthier, yet you did the same thing as soon as you could."

"It's not the same," Mya argued.

"No, you didn't leave a baby for someone else to raise," Corey said, "but you still left. Why?"

She was silent for a long time. So long that Corey wasn't sure she'd answer. Finally, she looked up at him and said, "I didn't want to get trapped." She shook her head. "I was just so afraid of getting stuck here and never getting the chance to experience life."

She turned and leaned against the railing, gripping the thick wooden beam. "I know there are dozens of things to love about living in a small town like Gauthier, but there is just so much out there, Corey. There are people who have spent their entire lives here without ever going anywhere else. That is insane."

"But it doesn't have to be one or the other," Corey said. He pointed back toward the law office. "Go in there and ask Carmen about the trip she and Scotty just took to New Zealand. Ask your grandmother about the cruise some of the ladies from her church are taking to the Bahamas." The swift flash of surprise on her face spoke volumes. "There's not an invisible wall keeping people trapped in Gauthier, Mya. You don't have to completely shut yourself off from this place." Corey paused, capturing her chin between his fingers and lifting her head as he added, "Or the people here who care about you."

She stared into his eyes, her grip on the beam so tight he knew it would leave indentations in her skin.

His gaze locked on her lips. He lowered his head and took her mouth in a slow-moving kiss. To his disappointment, she didn't let this one go on for nearly as long as their kiss in the library. Mya brought a hand to his jaw and moved his face away from hers.

"You've got to stop doing that," she said.

"But it's so much fun," Corey countered.

The stern look she shot his way was hampered by the laughter crinkling the corners of her eyes.

Her gaze roamed around the park again. "So, you think your baseball team can handle sprucing this place up? We're going to need to paint those park benches and prune a lot of the shrubbery."

"I think they can handle it," he said. "They're all going to be here early Saturday morning, with their gloves, shovels and trash bags."

"And their coach?" she asked.

The corner of his mouth tipped up in a smile. "Their coach will be leading the way."

"Hmm . . . I think their coach deserves a special reward for all his hard work. I may have to sweet-talk Aunt Mo into making her special oatmeal-raisin cookies you used to love so much."

"I've got a better idea," he said. "How about you let their coach take you to dinner?" Corey's chest constricted as he waited for her answer. "Come on, Mya," he urged when he saw the indecision in her eyes. He took her fingers and brought them to his lips, pressing one single, gentle kiss to her soft skin. "Let me take you to dinner."

An interminable stretch of time passed before she finally nodded.

"I think I'd like that."

CHAPTER 8

Mya slathered sunscreen on her arms, legs and face, then pulled her grandfather's tattered New Orleans Saints sun visor low on her forehead.

"Aunt Mo, are you almost done?" she called.

"In a minute," Maureen hollered.

Mya left the hall bathroom and headed for the front of the house. Her grandmother was waiting at the door, a straw hat with a wide brim atop her head.

"Well, it looks as if you're ready." Mya tugged on the green ribbon dangling from the hat.

"I sure am." Her grandmother hefted her purse over her shoulder. "Even though I'm only allowed to hand out bottles of water."

"With the way that sun is shining, you'll be the most popular person on Main Street." Mya laughed.

"Okay, let's get to it," Maureen said as

she entered the room wearing a paint-stained chambray shirt and a pair of jean cutoffs Mya was sure were older than she was.

They piled into the car and headed toward downtown Gauthier. As they edged closer to Main Street, Mya looked at the cars that lined both sides of Pecan Drive.

"Do you think all of these are volunteers?" she asked, but neither her grandmother nor Aunt Mo needed to answer. The proof revealed itself as soon as they crossed over Shoal Creek Lane. Volunteers cluttered the sidewalks, with rakes and shovels and buckets in hand.

"Oh, my God," Grandma breathed from the passenger seat.

"Don't cry," Mya told her, even though her throat instantly tightened at the show of support from the residents of Gauthier. She was suddenly overcome with pride. It felt strange to have such strong feelings for a place she'd written off for so many years, but how could she not feel a kinship with this town and its people?

"This is amazing," Mya said on an awe-filled breath.

She drove the full length of Main Street. The slanted parking spots in front of the buildings had been cordoned off by yellow caution tape, so she dropped her grandmother and Aunt Mo in front of Claudette's Beauty Parlor and drove down to Clark Street to park. She grabbed the pair of gloves she'd taken from her grandfather's gardening shed, along with a red-and-blue paisley scarf that she tucked into her back pocket.

Mya spotted Corey just outside of the Gauthier Pharmacy and Feed Store. He held a clipboard in one hand and a bullhorn in the other and looked every bit the high school coach. He called out a string of last names and gave those players instructions to wash the windows of Mike's Barbershop. The next set was ordered to add a fresh coat of paint to the porch railing surrounding Gauthier Savings and Loan, and yet another group of players was assigned to sand the outdoor deck of Emile's Restaurant.

Mya sidled up to Corey and tapped him on the shoulder.

He turned with the bullhorn to his mouth, primed to bellow out more instructions. He dropped it and smiled at her.

"Good morning," he said.

"Good morning to you. I see you already have things running like a well-oiled machine. How long have you been out here?"

"Since about six. I know we told volunteers to be here at eight, but I wanted to make sure everything was in place so people could get to work as soon as they arrived. I had Manny rope off the entire street because a buddy of mine has an old paint striper and agreed to come over and restripe the parking spots." He pointed across the street. "The Ladies' Auxiliary has already started pruning the shrubs in Heritage Park, and the football booster club is working on the old antiques store."

Mya surveyed the bevy of activity surrounding her. "I'm just surprised at how many people are willing to give up their Saturday morning to help out."

"I'm not," Corey said. "People love this town."

"Well, I'm proud of them all the same."

"You should be proud that you played such a key role in getting this done."

She looked over at him and smiled, her breath hitching a little at how breathtakingly gorgeous he was in his shades.

Corey glanced down at his clipboard, then back up at her. "So, are you ready to get to work? According to my list you're on sidewalk duty."

She barked out a laugh. "Put me to work, Coach."

Two hours later, Mya was ready to crawl under the wooden deck in front of Emile's Restaurant and take a nap. She lived a pretty active lifestyle, but her body wasn't used to continuous manual labor. Accompanied by several members of the Gauthier Fighting Lions cheerleading squad and drill team, she had pulled all the weeds popping out of the brick sidewalk that lined either side of Main Street. Her back ached from the constant crouching.

Mya walked over to the table where her grandmother sat, along with Clementine Washington. They were shaded by a green-and-white tent with *Gauthier Fighting Lions* printed on all four sides.

"Looks like you can use something cool to drink," her grandmother said. "You want water or punch?" She pointed to the orange coolers that were commonly seen hoisted over the heads of winning football coaches just before the game clock ticked down to zero.

"Water is fine," Mya answered, and was handed a blessedly cold bottle of water from a huge ice chest.

"Main Street is looking better already," her grandmother said. "I'll bet we'll have this place cleaned up by the end of the day."

Even though Main Street was well preserved, before this morning Mya was sure they were going to need more than just one day to spruce up this area. But with the more than one hundred volunteers working tirelessly, the idea of them being done by the end of the day didn't seem out of the realm of possibility.

Phylicia was moving methodically from parking spot to parking spot, pressure-washing oil and other automotive fluid that had leaked from cars and stained the asphalt. Aunt Mo led the group of volunteers who were adding a glossy coat of black paint to the wrought-iron lampposts that lined the street.

Her grandmother was right; this place was already looking better, and it wasn't even ten o'clock yet. Mya could not suppress the current of prideful satisfaction that rippled through her. This was happening because of *her.*

"You slacking off?"

Mya jumped and turned, finding Corey standing just a foot behind her. A swath of sweat stained the front of his green T-shirt and clung to his viciously ripped chest and stomach. Mya took a long pull on her water bottle, but it didn't cool off her heated body one bit.

"C'mere." Corey gestured with his head

and tugged at her sleeve.

"What?" Mya staggered behind him.

"I've got something to show you."

They walked along the side of the pharmacy and Mya knew where they were going before they reached the rear of the building.

The storage shed.

It was a small wooden structure, no more than six-by-eight feet, and used to store cleaning equipment and oversize boxes. There was just enough room for two horny teenagers to get into all kinds of trouble. Mya's skin tingled at the memories.

"Remember this?" Corey asked, retrieving a key from his pocket.

"Where did you get that key?"

"Told Shelly I needed to borrow a couple of buckets," he said. He opened the door to the darkened shed, and Mya's heart skipped several beats.

"All this sun must have gone to your head, Corey Anderson. You're crazy if you think I'm going in there with you."

He leaned close and buried his face against her neck, inhaling deep. "Come on, Peaches. You know you want to."

A double fudge brownie sundae with extra fudge was easier to resist than that invitation, but then the sundae was no good for her either. Mya took a step back, but Corey grabbed her wrist and pulled her into the shed. He shut the door, leaving them in the dark except for the light streaming in through the wooden slats of the walls.

He pushed aside an empty box, picked her up by the waist and planted her on the shelf that lined the shed's right wall. Mya's legs opened automatically to let Corey in, the height of the shelf bringing their bodies into perfect alignment. It was just as she remembered. Fifteen years ago, they wouldn't have even bothered to get undressed. Corey would have just moved her panties to the side and plunged inside of her in a matter of seconds.

"God, I used to live for this," Corey murmured against her neck. He ran his hands up and down her back then moved to her hips, encasing her thighs in his palms. "I would count down the minutes until three o'clock, when Doc Landry would leave to go check on that parrot. I knew as soon as his car pulled out of the alleyway that we had exactly twenty minutes."

"After that stupid bird died, I had to come up with all kinds of excuses to leave the store." Mya laughed.

"You got pretty good at it," Corey mused.

"I still can't believe he never realized what we were up to. I used to be so scared we'd get caught."

"I was way too good to ever get caught." He rubbed his nose along the edge of her jaw, his lips grazing her neck and collarbone with soft kisses.

"Corey, stop it," Mya said with the weakest, most pitiful protest she'd ever uttered. "There are over a hundred people out here. We can't do this right now."

"Nobody knows we're in here."

Bare fingers clutched the small of her back and Mya's entire being tingled at the sensation of his rough warmth abrading her skin. He pulled her into closer contact with his body, his hands moving down to grip her backside.

She buried her hands underneath his shirt. He was divine; smooth skin draped over solid firmness. Mya clawed her way up his back, remembering the way the ropy muscles in his shoulders would undulate against her hands as he pumped in and out of her body with swift, sure strokes. He could light her on fire in mere seconds and bring her to earth-shattering orgasm moments later. She'd slept with a total of four men in her thirty-two years, and not one of them had ever come close to satisfying her the way Corey had.

Mya let her head fall back as Corey's

hands traveled from her waist to her stomach, then up and over her satin-and-lace bra. He hooked his fingers just over the edge of the cups and pulled them down. Her nipples hardened in anticipation. When his roughened palms closed over her breasts, a whimper escaped her throat.

Corey groaned against her neck, licking and sucking and biting as his fingers pinched and plucked and rubbed her distended nipples.

"I really want to pull those shorts off of you," he whispered against her skin, "but I locked my wallet in the glove compartment of my car." He pulled away from her neck and looked at her. "You don't happen to have a condom on you, do you?"

"Why would I have a condom?" Mya asked.

"Thought not," he said with a sigh. "Dammit, Mya. How am I supposed to go back out there like this?"

She looked down and her mouth watered at the sight of the huge erection pulsing just on the other side of his zippered khaki shorts.

"You're the one who started this," she said. He still held her naked breasts in his palms, and she wasn't inclined to move his hands away. Having his rough skin upon

171

her felt like heaven.

Corey lowered his forehead to hers and gently squeezed her breasts. "If I don't have you soon I think I might die."

A wry grin eased up the corners of her lips. How many times had she heard that line from him?

"That may have worked back in high school," Mya said. "But I'm not as naive as I used to be." She clamped on to his forearms and pulled his hands away, then straightened her bra back into place and smoothed the wrinkles from her shirt.

"I'm not playing around, Mya. This is killing me."

As she watched him struggle with his unfulfilled lust, all Mya could think about was her own valiant attempt to resist the hunger that had been building within her. It was a losing battle. Her body had been teetering along the edge of desire for the past two weeks, and the ache became harder to fight with every second she was around him.

She was tired of fighting.

She was no longer a love-struck teenager. She knew exactly what she would be getting herself into if she embarked upon a sexual relationship with Corey. It would be in direct opposition to the claim she'd made a long time ago that she was over him. She was setting herself up for frustration, possibly even heartache.

But there was one thing she was certain to get: pleasure. Much, *much* pleasure.

Streaks of filtering sunlight sliced across his chest, highlighting the way his moist shirt clung to his well-defined six-pack. The impulse to strip the shirt from his body and lick her way up and down his torso was so strong that Mya knew she had to break free right now. If they stayed in here much longer, they would both end up naked, sweaty and panting.

But satisfied. So incredibly, remarkably satisfied.

Corey stepped up to her again and captured her mouth in a swift kiss. She bit back a moan and pulled away.

"We need to get back out there," she said, putting her hands on his chest and gently pushing him.

He let out a low curse as he backed up. His eyes zeroed in on her nipples that puckered against her cotton shirt, and he licked those lips that Mya wished were still exploring her neck.

Corey's head fell back as he let out another groan. He cupped his straining erection and squeezed himself through the fabric. The picture of sexual frustration.

"Just like high school," Mya said, unable to keep the laughter from her voice.

"This isn't funny," he gritted through clenched teeth. "Do you know how hard it will be to work like this for the rest of the day?"

Mya empathized with him, but not enough to help ease his . . . situation. She scooted off the shelf, brushing against Corey in the tight confines of the storage shed. Her blood heated at the contact, and she knew she needed to get out fast.

She pointed a finger at Corey's chest. "Remember, we're supposed to be working. Don't try luring me away again."

He slid a knowing gaze her way and smiled with deliberate slyness. "You could have said no."

Yeah, right. When had she ever been able to say no to him?

"I mean it, Corey Anderson. You're not going to tempt me again today."

A hint of challenge entered his eyes, and Mya knew she'd just landed herself into a heap of trouble.

"You willing to bet on that?" Corey asked.

She refused to take the bait. It would only give him incentive to try harder, and she didn't need Corey laying on the heavy charm. The day was hot enough.

Her hand on the rusty door handle, Mya pointed at him again and said, "Stay away." Then she cut out of the storage shed before he lured her back in.

Corey hitched a heel on the rim of the shovel and drove it deep into the packed earth, turning up the dirt at the base of the oak tree. Sweat poured off him, and his muscles were so tired they quivered, but he continued to ram the shovel. He had enough pent-up energy to till this entire damn park.

Why had he dragged Mya into that storage shed?

He'd known what would happen — he'd get worked up. And he'd also known what *wouldn't* happen — sex. Of any kind. They were in the middle of cleaning up Main Street, for God's sake. The kids from his baseball team were swarming around this place. He knew better than to try having sex in a storage shed.

Seeing that tiny building again and having Mya so close by had caused something in his brain to snap. He'd lived out too many fantasies in that cluttered shed to pass up the opportunity to revisit a few of them. What he hadn't counted on was Mya's reaction. If only she hadn't responded to his touch the way she had, maybe then he could get his body under control.

"Dammit," Corey grunted with another vicious thump of the shovel.

Every time he came close to cooling off from the fire she'd lit within him, he'd feel her nipples pebble against his palms, a phantom imprint that wouldn't go away. She'd been ready for him. If she had been wearing a skirt today instead of those shorts, he would have been inside of her, condom or no condom.

Although, a skirt wouldn't cup her perfectly rounded butt the way those shorts did, and he wouldn't have the view he had right now.

Balancing a begonia bulb in one hand, Mya bent over and settled it in the dirt he'd turned over around the base of another oak tree about twenty feet away. She tapped the dirt around it and motioned for one of the cheerleaders carrying an old-fashioned tin watering can to come over and moisten the soil. When the girl was done, Mya planted her gloved fists on her hips and looked around the park. Her eyes caught his and she smiled.

God, he'd missed her smile. Even on his worst day, when Coach had drilled his ass in practice or he'd gotten caught up with his idiot brothers in some kind of trouble-making scheme, one smile from Mya would change his entire outlook. So much time had passed, yet the feelings he'd had for her still ran as strong as ever. He'd never gotten over her.

And Corey realized he never wanted to.

Mya Dubois had stolen his heart a long time ago, and he was all too willing to let her keep it, provided she allowed the rest of him to come along for the ride.

She walked up to him, those hands still on her hips, the top half of her face shaded by that ratty black-and-gold sun visor.

"I thought you were avoiding me for the rest of the day," Corey said.

"I think you've had enough time to cool down," she said.

"Think again," Corey muttered. "I'm as bad as these horny baseball players running behind the cheerleaders."

"We've had our turn at that."

"There's nothing saying we can't have it again." Corey saw the desire in her eyes. She wanted to, but damn if she wasn't fighting it.

"Are you almost done here?" she asked. "We need to get those flower bulbs in the ground, then we need to clean out the fish pond. I ordered twenty Japanese koi fish for the pond, my contribution to the town of Gauthier."

"Koi? That had to set you back a few hundred dollars," he said.

Mya shrugged. "I may not be rolling in dough, but I do okay. I want this place to impress the media at the end of the month. And with the progress we've made today, it's going to do just that."

"It does look good," Corey said, trailing his eyes over the park.

Most of the shrubbery had been pruned, and new flowers had been planted around the base of most of the oak trees that lined the pathway leading to the waterwheel and wooden gazebo. The park benches were in the process of getting a fresh coat of paint and piles of raked leaves and pine needles were being loaded into huge wheelbarrows. They would be turned into mulch and brought back to help fertilize the soil around the newly planted flowers.

"Lunch!" someone called. "We've got lunch!"

"Lunch?" Corey looked over at Mya, but she only shrugged her shoulders with a confused frown crinkling her forehead. They walked out of the park entrance and found dozens of people gathered around Jamal's top-of-the-line pickup truck. His friend stood in the truck bed, handing out sandwiches.

"He bought lunch for everyone?" Mya asked, awe in her voice.

"That's Jamal," Corey said.

"Hey," Jamal called out to Corey. "I've got cases of potato chips in the front. Come and give me a hand."

Corey took his gloves off and handed them to Mya. He gestured back toward the park. "Meet me in the gazebo in fifteen minutes. I'll bring lunch." He winked at her and headed to the chaos surrounding Jamal's truck.

CHAPTER 9

Mya sat on the freshly sanded porch steps in front of Emile's Restaurant, unabashedly watching Corey as he helped to serve the lunch his friend had so generously provided. The way the damp T-shirt molded to Corey's back made her mouth instantly water.

She blew out a defeated sigh. Her body's demands had waged an all-out war against her common sense, and her common sense was ready to concede. The fight was futile and, at this point, exhausting.

Why should she deny herself any longer? It's not as if she were in danger of falling for Corey's charm again. It's not as if sleeping with him would tether her to this town. In two weeks, after they held the 175th-year celebration and convinced the historical society and state tourism board that Gauthier was worthy of their attention, she would be on a plane to New York. Why not head back to the Big Apple a sexually satisfied woman?

"I see some things haven't changed." Phylicia plopped down on the step next to her.

"Why do you say that?" Mya asked, though the answer was obvious. She was blatantly staring at the man, and if anyone knew the intimacies of her previous relationship with Corey, it was Phylicia. The only thing Mya hadn't shared with her best friend was news of the baby she'd miscarried.

"He does still look good," Phylicia mused. "He was cutting your grandmother's lawn the other day, and pulled his shirt off just as I drove by. I damn near wrecked my truck."

Mya belted out a laugh so loud it drew stares.

"That friend of his is pretty hot, too," Phil commented.

"Jamal?" Mya dragged her eyes away from Corey long enough to glance at the other man. Yep, gorgeous just about summed him up.

"I did some work at that house he's fixing up. I almost had a heart attack when I walked in there and saw Sheetrock on the walls," Phil said with a derisive grunt.

"I got the grand tour earlier this week. I know it probably kills you to see him get rid of some of the original structure, but that house is going to be spectacular when he's done."

"*If* he's ever done," Phil snorted. "He's been working on it for months. Hey, do you want a sandwich?"

Mya couldn't keep the coyness from seeping through her voice. "I've already got a lunch date."

Phil gasped and twisted toward her. "Girl, are you thinking of giving Corey the booty again?"

"My goodness, Phylicia, would you shut up! Or at least keep your voice down," she said with a terse whisper.

"Mya Eloise Dubois!" Mya had never heard her name draped in such righteous indignation. "I am appalled."

"What's the big deal?" She shrugged. "It's not as if I haven't slept with him before."

"That's not what's appalling," Phil said. "It's the fact that you've been back in Gauthier for two weeks and you're already getting some. I've been in this damn town my entire life and the only action I get these days is from my friend Bob."

Mya searched her memory, but couldn't come up with anyone. "Who's Bob?" she had to ask.

"My battery-operated boyfriend," Phil

drawled.

Mya looked over at her friend and burst out laughing. As beautiful as she was, Phil had always had a hard time when it came to guys. Mya was convinced that Phil's problems stemmed from her job. She confused men. It was hard to reconcile the varnish-stained overalls with the amazingly gorgeous woman who wore them.

"You should know better than to wait for the guy to make the first move. If it's been that long, why don't you ask someone out?" Mya suggested, picking up her bottled water.

"It's not worth the bother." Phil stood and dusted her backside. "Bob has an attachment that connects to the power drill. There's not a man in Gauthier who can compete with that."

Mya started choking on the water she'd just swallowed.

Phil didn't even blink. She said, "I'm going to see a man about a sandwich. I'll catch up with you later." And she headed toward the pickup truck.

Ten minutes later, Mya was still trying to get thoughts of power tools and friends named Bob out of her mind, when Corey sidled up to her carrying two wrapped sandwiches and two bags of chips.

"I thought you were meeting me in the gazebo?" he asked.

Mya shook her head and patted the sanded step next to her. "Too secluded. I thought this was safer."

"In my experience, safer is never as much fun." He settled onto the porch step and handed her the promised turkey sandwich.

"It was sweet of Jamal to buy lunch for everyone. That must have set him back a pretty penny."

"He can afford it," Corey said, biting into his sandwich. He swallowed and continued, "Jamal is a trust-fund kid. His family owns one of the largest construction firms in Phoenix."

"Yet he's working as an assistant coach at a small-town high school?"

"He's not on the staff. He's just helping me out with the team while he works on the business plan for an architectural firm he wants to open. We were teammates back at Arizona State," Corey added.

Mya's eyes drifted over to the man who was leaning against his truck surrounded by a group of teens. She recognized the hero worship in the eyes of the young girls. Jamal Johnson was prime teenage-crush material.

"He *is* gorgeous," Mya commented.

"Hey, I'm sitting right here. You want to

squash the lusting after my best friend?"

She glanced at Corey and laughed. "I'm just admiring him from afar. It looks as if he's got his hands full." She bit into her sandwich and followed it with a couple of chips. "So," Mya said after she'd swallowed, "how much more do you think we can get done before the rain rolls in?"

Corey looked up at the sky, where thick clouds were stalking in from the south. "With the way that sky looks, we'll be lucky if we have another hour."

"I hope the lampposts Aunt Mo and her crew painted this morning will be okay."

"If not, I'll keep practice short this coming Tuesday and Wednesday and bring the team out here to retouch whatever paint the rain messes up." His gaze roamed their surroundings. "With all the volunteers that showed up today, we were able to get more done than I'd anticipated."

"It's been amazing," Mya agreed.

Corey nudged her leg with his knee. "You know what would make it even more amazing?"

Mya brought her hand up. "Don't finish that sentence. You are worse than you were back in high school."

"I used to get more action back in high school," he said. "If I knew back then that I would eventually go this long without sex, I probably would have killed myself." He finished off his sandwich and balled up the plastic wrap and empty potato chip bag.

Mya told herself to let his statement pass, but she couldn't help herself. "How long has it been?"

Corey reached over and grabbed the empty remnants of her lunch. With a wicked grin, he said, "Long enough that you should take this as a warning. Once we get started, I may not be able to stop."

Okay. So that was promising.

Mya squeezed her legs tight and pleaded with her heart to slow the heck down. She still had plenty of time to make sure Corey came through on his promise.

The rain held off for another two hours, but when it started it was as if someone had cracked a glass jar filled with water over their heads. People scrambled for cover under the awnings that shaded some of the entrances to businesses on Main Street. Others huddled in the wooden gazebo in Heritage Park or inside some of the stores that were open.

After a few minutes, the torrential downpour slowed to a slight but steady shower. The volunteers began venturing out into the rain, covering their heads with plastic garbage bags as they swiftly made their way to their cars. Mya didn't bother shielding herself from the rain. She was already soaked.

She went over to the tent where her grandmother had spent most of the day handing out water and sports drinks.

"Looks like God decided we'd done enough work," Grandma said.

"He kept it nice and dry for most of the day," Mya replied. "Why don't you pack up your things? I'll find Aunt Mo."

"She already left," her grandmother informed her. "She banged her knee against one of those steel posts in front of the barbershop and howled like a fool."

"Is she okay?" Mya asked.

Her grandmother waved off her concern. "I think it was just an excuse to leave. Anyway, I'm going over to Clementine's. Some of the girls are getting together to play cards. She'll drive me home. Do you need a ride?"

"No, I'm good," Mya said. She pointed a warning finger at her grandmother. "Remember, no sweets or sugary sodas for you. Make sure she doesn't eat the wrong foods, Mrs. Washington."

Her grandmother rolled her eyes, but didn't argue. Mya kissed her cheek and dashed back out into the rain. She headed for Phil's truck, which was parked in the alley between the pharmacy and the bank, but Corey intercepted her. He stepped out from where he'd been helping Jamal load shovels and rakes into the bed of his truck and grabbed her by the waist. He pulled her up against him, her back crushed to his front.

"Where do you think you're going?" he growled into her ear.

"I was . . . uh, going to see if Phil could give me a ride home," she said.

She felt Corey's jaw move against her neck as he shook his head. "You don't need Phil to give you a ride."

His husky voice caused a fissure of need to split her heart wide open. Mya melted against him. "Then let me at least say goodbye to her," Mya said.

"Be back here in five minutes," he told her.

She made it back in three.

Following Corey, she jogged over to his SUV parked just a few yards away on Maurepas Drive. He opened the passenger door and helped her into the passenger seat, then popped open the glove compartment and retrieved his wallet. There was a condom in there, and they were going to put it to use within the hour.

Mya swallowed the knot of lust that lodged in her throat. "How far from here do you live?" she asked as soon as Corey shut his door.

"Ten minutes." He rammed the key in the ignition and started the truck. "But I can make it there in seven."

"Do that," she said.

Corey backed out of his parking spot and continued up Maurepas and onto the highway. They turned into a subdivision that had been nothing but acres of sugarcane fields the last time Mya had been to this part of town. Despite being a planned community, the houses still had huge yards instead of the postage-stamp properties that usually comprised this type of neighborhood.

Corey turned into the driveway of a sprawling two-story home that was way too big for just one person. He drove past the house and into a backyard that was surrounded by high fencing. He parked just outside a detached garage.

"Sorry I have to park in the rain," he said. "The garage is filled with a bunch of Jamal's crap that he's storing here while he works on his house."

"It's okay," Mya answered with a husky breath. "I'm already soaking wet."

Corey squeezed his fingers around the steering wheel and cursed. In a strained voice, he said, "Are you trying to make me finish before we even get started?"

"I'm sorry," she lied.

"Get out of the truck," he said between gritted teeth.

Mya hopped out of the SUV and ran around the back. Corey caught her arm and pulled her against him. He was soaked, the fabric plastered to his chiseled chest. He attacked her mouth with hungry kisses, plowing past her closed lips and plunging his tongue inside. Mya responded with hunger of her own, clasping her hands behind his head and holding him securely to her.

Her brain faintly registered the inground swimming pool and teak wood cabana, along with the towering magnolia trees shading his massive backyard. It was exquisite and, like the house, too large for a single person.

As she felt Corey's iron-hard erection rise up against her stomach she put the house and every other thought out of her mind.

"We're not making it inside," he said roughly against her neck. He stopped under the leafy branches of a magnolia tree and tore the shirt over his head.

"Corey, what are you doing?"

"Strip," he ordered as he unsnapped his shorts and shucked them down his legs.

Mya's mouth gaped open even as her hands went for the hem of her shirt. "Are we really going to have sex outside in the rain?"

"Damn right," Corey said. He grabbed her and brought her body flush against his own. "Don't worry," he said, unzipping her shorts and pulling them down. "The neighbors are too far away to see into the backyard. I skinny-dip in the pool all the time."

The mental picture that statement elicited sent a streak of fire racing through her bloodstream. Mya sighed into his kiss, her body fever-hot despite the rain falling in fits and spurts through the leafy branches.

His mouth never leaving hers, Corey lowered her to the ground. He unhooked her bra and pulled the soaked fabric from her shoulders and down her arms, following the path with his mouth. He tunneled his fingers underneath the rim of her panties and guided them over her thighs and down her legs.

Their rain-slicked bodies moved easily against each other. Corey cradled her waist and hoisted her up so that she straddled his lap. She bent over and drew her mouth across his chest, flicking at his flat nipple and softly biting his wet skin. He hissed with pleasure, running his palms down her spine, settling them at the small of her back.

"Grab those shorts," he ordered. "My wallet is in the back pocket."

Mya scooted up his torso and reached for the shorts he'd kicked off a few feet away. She let out a shocked gasp when Corey lifted his head and covered her core with his mouth. He palmed her backside, holding her in place as his tongue delved, solid and deep, into her slick flesh.

The moan that escaped her lips was animalistic. Mya arched her back, bringing her center closer to his foraging tongue.

Tension gripped low in her belly, pulsing hot and fevered with every lick and plunge. She encased the sides of his face between her thighs, pumping her body in rhythm to his mouth.

"Oh, my God," she moaned as she leaned back and gripped his thighs. He flicked his tongue against her clitoris, fast and furious, curling around the swollen bud and pulling it into his mouth. Then two of his fingers swept in from behind and slipped into her soaking body.

The climax that had started building within her blood erupted with a ferocity that had her screaming toward the sky.

Corey captured her by the waist before she could collapse and laid her onto the soaked bed of soft grass. With a satisfied smile on those incredibly talented lips, he grabbed the condom she'd dropped and ripped it open. After covering himself with the latex, he spread her legs apart and entered her with one long, deep, decadent stroke.

Mya's world exploded. Everything ceased to exist, except for this one man who had stolen her heart so many years ago. As he moved with deliberate slowness, driving his hard flesh deeper into her with every thrust, she closed her eyes and melted into the moment. She didn't need anything else. Only Corey, loving her body the way no other man ever could.

Mya wrapped her legs around his back and locked him on top of her, her hands gripping his rain-slicked shoulders. She sank her fingers into his flesh as he started to pump faster.

He emitted a clipped, low grunt with each thrust, rocking into her body, setting her entire world on fire. Mya clung to him, savoring every delicious slide of his hard flesh inside of her.

The sensation that started as a small kernel in her belly sprouted into the most intense, magnificent orgasm her body had ever experienced. Corey continued to plunge into her, quickening his thrusts, wrenching another skin-tingling climax from her just moments after the first.

Mya collapsed onto the grass, her body humming with the kind of satisfaction she had not felt in fifteen years.

"Oh, God," she sighed. She stared up at Corey, a slow smile pulling at her lips. "That was better than I remembered."

Corey burrowed his head into the pillow, wanting nothing more than to stay tangled in these sheets with Mya for the rest of the morning. He reached his hand out in search of her warm skin, but came up with nothing but cool, silk sheets.

What the . . . ?

He sprang up from the bed, tossing the pillows and sheets onto the floor. He looked around the room, a sense of foreboding washing over him as he searched the bathroom, then ventured downstairs.

Empty. The entire house was empty. Mya had actually left him in bed.

The elegant string of curses that tore forth from him was reminiscent of his ballplaying days, but the ire stirring in his gut right now was ten times worse than anything he'd felt after a bad call by an umpire. How in the hell could she leave him? After everything that had passed between them last night?

Corey went to the laundry room and snatched clothes from the dryer. He violently jammed his arms into a clean T-shirt and pulled on a pair of worn jeans. He shoved his feet into his tennis shoes, then grabbed his keys from where he'd tossed them on the kitchen counter.

As he backed out of the driveway, he eyed the massive magnolia tree in his backyard and his stomach clenched in remembrance of all they had done underneath those branches. If he could, he would have the damn thing bronzed.

He turned out of his driveway and headed for the Dubois house.

Ten minutes later, Corey pulled up to the wooden fence surrounding Eloise Dubois's yard. His chest tightened at the sight of Mya. She was hanging sheets on the clothesline that stretched across the side yard, just beyond the vegetable garden.

She jumped when he closed his car door, and spun around. Standing with a flowered sheet folded over her arm, guilt was written all over her face as he approached.

"Hi," she said.

"That's it?" Corey asked.

"Corey, let's not do this."

"After what we did last night you had better believe we're doing this. Mya, if you think I'm going to let you stand there and tell me last night meant nothing, you're crazy."

"I didn't say that it meant nothing, but don't make it out to mean any more than it did, either. We had sex. Fine. It's not as if we haven't done that before. But now that we've gotten it out of our systems, we need to just go back to working on the celebration."

"I haven't gotten you out of my system, and I don't plan to," he said.

"Corey, please." She let out a tired sigh and kneaded the bridge of her nose. He captured her arm, forcing her to drop the sheet. "Goodness! What!" she shouted, jerking her arm away.

"Why is it so hard for you to say it, Mya?"

"What, Corey? What do you want me to say?"

"That you still have feelings for me. And not the kind of feelings one night of sex will take care of. It's more than that. I can feel it. I felt it last night."

Her eyes closed again. Corey tried not to be offended by the anguish that was evident on her face, but it wasn't easy. Why in the hell was this so difficult for her to accept? They were good together. They always had been. If not for his one indiscretion all those years ago, who knows where he and Mya would be today?

One thing he did know, he was not letting her slip away so easily this time. He'd made that mistake once, and it had cost him fifteen years of living without the woman he loved. He didn't want to lose another second.

Corey captured both her wrists and pulled her close, pressing a light kiss on the back of her hand.

"I've loved you more than half my life, Mya. I know you think that's crazy since it seems like a lifetime since we've seen each other, but it doesn't change the way I've felt about you all these years. No one has ever measured up to you. Not even close."

Her bottom lip trembled, and she pulled it between her teeth. When she spoke, her voice cracked with emotion. "Corey, what do you want from me?"

"I want you to give this a chance, Mya. Give *us* a chance. I don't want just one night with you."

"I'm not sure I can give you more than that," she answered.

Corey's shoulders sank. Why was she so

hardheaded?

"I need to finish this," she said, stooping low to pick up another sheet. "And I promised Aunt Mo I would help her sew the skirting for the main stage, so I won't be able to come with you to New Orleans to listen to that band tonight."

"Is this how it's going to be?" he asked.

She didn't say anything else, just resumed clipping the sheet on the line with the old-fashioned wooden clothespins.

Corey stood there for a moment with his hands on his hips, astounded that one woman could possess such stubbornness. He knew better than to press her. She would only close herself off even more.

He bit back a curse as he turned and headed back to his SUV. He sat behind the wheel for several long moments, just staring at her, knowing it made her uncomfortable.

Good. He wanted her rattled — more than she already was.

He could think of only one reason for her to have sneaked out of his bed the way she had this morning: she had been just as blown away at what they'd shared as he had been. The bond between him and Mya had always been powerful, but last night had been . . . otherworldly. It was too potent to deny. But she was trying, and Corey knew her well enough to know she would only try harder.

The clock was ticking. Gauthier's anniversary celebration was only two weeks away and he could sense that she was planning to head back to New York as soon as it was over. Corey didn't know how he would do it, but he was going to get through to Mya before it was too late.

CHAPTER 10

"One strawberry daiquiri with an extra shot of rum," Phylicia said as she placed a bowl-shaped wineglass in front of Mya. She poured the remaining slushy mixture into another wineglass, hitting the side of the blender until every drop came tumbling out.

"I think you've got it all." Mya chuckled.

Phil peered into the empty pitcher. "Just making sure. After the week I've had I can use whatever form of relaxation I can get."

"Why? What's going on?"

"Nothing I'm going to bore you with, especially when I know we've got much more interesting things to talk about."

"You mean the plans for the anniversary celebration?" Mya asked with a sarcastic grunt. She knew exactly what Phil wanted to talk about, but Mya wasn't up for it. She'd spent much of the day trying to push Corey Anderson and his amazing sexual skills out of her mind.

Phylicia gave her the evil eye, something she was notoriously good at. "Start talking."

"You picked me up from his house this morning, Phil. There's not much else to say."

"Mya Eloise Dubois, if you don't start talking right now, I am marching straight to your grandmother's and telling her what you and Corey used to do in her house when she and your grandpa would drive to town."

She cut her eyes at Phil. "You so do not play fair."

"I never claimed to. Now spill," Phylicia said, scooting onto the bar stool in the modern kitchen/living/dining area that Mya would never have imagined her best friend living in. For someone whose entire life revolved around restoring historic homes, Phylicia's modest cookie-cutter house was a downright contradiction. The first time Mya had walked through the door, her jaw had literally dropped open.

Mya glanced over at the one person she'd shared almost every secret and dream with and knew she wouldn't be able to hold anything back. Problem was she didn't know where to start.

Actually, knowing Phil, she *did* know where to start.

"The sex was great," she opened with. "Seriously, *seriously* great."

"I'll bet." Phil smiled as she took a sip of her frozen daiquiri. "I won't make you go into detail because we're grown-ups now. Unless, of course, you want to."

Mya rolled her eyes.

"Okay, okay." Phil held up her hands. "So, now that we've established that the sex was great, why exactly did you call me at the butt crack of dawn to come and pick you up from his house?"

"Because, Phil." Mya shoved an agitated hand through her springy curls and massaged her scalp. The persistent throb that had been hounding her since she'd crept out of Corey's bed like some thief in the night continued to pound.

"I can't go there again with Corey," she continued. "What we had ended a long time ago. I'm a completely different person. So is he."

"So, how do *those* two people feel about each other?"

"What?" Mya asked.

"You just said that you're both two completely different people than you were back in high school. So, as two single adults, how — other than being sexually attracted to

202

each other — do you two feel about each other?"

Mya's eyelids slid shut. She tried to deny the admission she was about to make, but she knew she couldn't. Not after last night.

"I think I'm falling in love with him all over again," she said. She waited for Phil's response, but all she heard was the sound of the stool scraping on the ceramic floor. She opened her eyes to find Phil reaching inside a kitchen cabinet. "What are you doing?"

"Getting the shot glasses," Phylicia called over her shoulder. "This calls for some serious reinforcements. You want to stick with the rum or should I pull out the bourbon?"

"The rum is fine," Mya said.

They brought the half-full daiquiris, along with the bottle of rum and the shot glasses, into the living room and settled on the sofa. Yet both of their shot glasses remained dry as Mya poured her heart out to her best friend.

"I just don't know what to do, Phil. I mean, really, who does this?"

"Does what?"

"Carry a torch for the same boy for fifteen years."

"Give yourself a break, Mya. It's not as if you and Corey had some passing fling in high school. You two loved each other more than half the married couples I know. I was jealous as hell of what you two had back then. And, to be honest, I'm not the least bit surprised that you and Corey have landed right back here. If there are any two people who were meant to be together, it's you two."

Mya stared at Phylicia with blanket confusion on her face. "Who are you and what have you done with my best friend?"

Phil flipped her off. "I may not always show it, but I'm still a romantic at heart," she said. "Seriously, Mya, there has always been something special between you and Corey."

Mya cradled her forehead in her hand. "I know." She sighed. "That's what scares me the most. It feels as if I'm right back where I started." She shook her head at the ridiculousness of it. "Here I am, thirty-two years old and still pining for Corey."

"What are you going to do about it?"

"I don't know," Mya admitted. "It's not as if I can drop everything and move back to Gauthier. My life is in New York." Mya shoved her hand in her hair. "God, why am I even talking about this? It was one night. It's so typical of me to make things out to be bigger than they really are. I need to be more like you."

"What's that supposed to mean?" Phil asked with an affronted frown.

"You know what I mean. You never got all emotional and stuff over guys."

"That's because they avoided me like head lice. Are you forgetting the hours you spent in my bedroom while I moped about some loser who wouldn't give me the time of day?"

Mya reached over and captured Phil's hand. "You didn't have the easiest time when it came to dating. But, from what I hear, now the opposite is true. Aunt Mo said you're the queen of playing hard-to-get."

A smile curled up the side of Phil's mouth. "I do get evil pleasure at turning them down. Do you know Roddy Palmer had the nerve to ask me to dinner a few weeks ago, as if he doesn't remember standing me up for the senior prom? I waited until he made reservations and everything before turning him down."

"Phylicia Phillips. When did you become such a tease?"

"It's something I've perfected over the years," Phil said. They both looked at each other and burst out laughing. Phil squeezed her hand. "I've missed you, Mya. It's been too long since we've done this."

A lump of guilt formed in Mya's throat at the longing she heard in her friend's voice.

"The phone calls and emails are nice and all, but it doesn't compare to having my best friend here with me," Phil continued. "Promise you won't stay away this long again."

"I won't. Promise."

They spent the next hour catching up. Phil pressed Mya for behind-the-scenes drama on the Broadway productions she had worked on for the past year, but Mya was more interested in learning about some of the houses Phylicia had helped to restore. Her friend's work was starting to gain national attention in the world of home restoration.

"I can't believe how much you've expanded your dad's business," Mya said.

Phil grimaced. "He's probably turning in his grave," she said as she reached for the bottle of rum and poured two fingers into her shot glass.

"Why would you say that?"

"Dad was not on board with my expansion ideas. He was content with working on the little fixer-uppers here in Gauthier. We had a huge fight about it just before he died."

Mya reached over and put a hand on her friend's shoulder. One of her biggest regrets was not coming back to Gauthier to attend Phil's father's funeral.

"I've never seen a man who doted on his daughter as much as your dad doted on you. Don't worry about some silly little fight. I know he's proud of what you've accomplished these past couple of years."

Phil sent her a strained, sad smile, and Mya's heart constricted even more. There was a pain in her friend's eyes that worried her.

"Well," Phil said, pushing up from the sofa, "now that we've officially turned this fun girls' night into a crying fest, I say we go all the way." She walked over to a beautiful mahogany cabinet that Mya had no doubts was once a resident of a junkyard before Phil got her hands on it. She opened it to reveal shelves lined with DVDs. She pulled out two slim cases and held them up.

"*Beaches* or *Steel Magnolias?*" Phil asked.

Mya expelled a wistful sigh as she pointed to the DVD in Phil's left hand. "Let's start with Bette Midler. I'll get the tissues."

"And I'll get more liquor," Phil said.

Mya carried the bushel of green beans up

207

the steps and set it on the folding table she'd set up on the back porch. She dragged the trash can from the kitchen and positioned it at the edge of the table.

As if they had sensed that she was ready, Aunt Mo's car pulled into the yard and her aunt and grandmother both exited the car. Grandma's hair bore the perfectly coiffed evidence of her weekly visit to Claudette's. Mya started to help her up the steps, but the look Grandma shot her had Mya snatching her hand back.

"I'll be out to help you with these beans in a minute," her grandmother said.

Maureen carried a brown grocery bag from the car.

"Is there more?" Mya asked.

"Nope, this is it," Maureen said as she ascended the back porch steps. Moments later she was walking down the steps, sans bag. "I need to get back to work. I'm already twenty minutes past the end of my lunch break."

Her grandmother walked out onto the porch carrying two glasses of iced tea. "Did she say that I made her late?" her grandmother asked, gesturing toward Maureen's car as it backed out of the yard.

"Not specifically," Mya said.

"Good, because I didn't make her late.

She was the one who couldn't stop running her mouth in Claudette's shop. She and Claudette are like oil and water."

Mya grinned at the mental picture. She sat at the table, and together she and her grandmother started snapping the edges off the beans. They put the stalks in a huge, dented stainless-steel bowl that Mya remembered from her childhood.

"It's been a long time since I did this," Mya remarked.

"To tell you the truth, it's been a while since I did it, too. Once your grandfather retired, he took over all the canning and preserving. I used to call him Martha Stewart the Second."

"I can't even fathom it," Mya laughed.

"Oh, yes, honey. He would tie my apron around his waist and spend all day in front of the stove, heating the mason jars, filling them with brine, soaking them."

"Sorry I missed seeing that," Mya said.

"So am I," her grandmother replied.

The sad smile on her face caused Mya's heart to twist with guilt. She dropped the beans and reached for her grandmother's hand.

"I'm so sorry I stayed away for so long." Her voice broke, riddled with shame and remorse. "I honestly thought it was okay since I would fly you guys up to New York, but now I realize it wasn't the same."

"No, it was not," her grandmother said. "For a long time, I thought we had done something wrong. I know Elizabeth was always ashamed of us."

"No. Never," Mya said, shaking her head with such vehemence that the clip holding up her curls sprang free and dropped to the porch floor. "I have never been ashamed. You and Granddad gave me everything I could ever ask for, and I love you both so much for that. I am so sorry that you ever felt that way.

"I didn't leave Gauthier because of anything either of you did. I just . . . I wanted more," she said. "I love my life in New York, but I am sorry for not coming home more often."

Her grandmother placed a palm against Mya's cheek. "It's good to have you home."

Mya covered her hand and pressed her cheek more firmly against it. She couldn't staunch the flow of tears that started down her face. When she saw the telltale glistening in her grandmother's eyes, it just made her tears fall harder.

"Just look at us," her grandmother said. "Your grandfather is probably having a good laugh at the way we're carrying on."

"Knowing Granddad, he's shaking his head and muttering something about 'women' and 'emotional crap' under his breath." Mya sniffed.

"Well, he would be right this time."

They wiped their faces with a dishcloth and resumed snapping. Before long, the bowl was overflowing with fresh green beans.

"Did Aunt Mo remember to buy the brining salt?" Mya asked.

"I hope she did," Grandma said. "I'll check. Why don't you go in the shed and get the double boiler."

Mya went into the wooden storage shed behind the house and found the huge pot in the same place it had occupied for as long as she could remember. She grabbed the pot, along with the rack for canning.

"She didn't forget the salt," her grandmother announced as Mya mounted the steps.

"Good. I'll start boiling the water."

"Looks like we've got company," her grandmother said, motioning toward the road. Mya twisted around. A silver two-door Mercedes coupe pulled into the graveled driveway.

"Who's that?" she asked. She got her answer a second later when the door opened and Corey alighted from the car. He waved at them.

"Oh, great," she muttered. Mya pushed past her grandmother and went into the house. She pulled in several deep breaths as she tried to collect herself.

She'd managed to avoid Corey the entire week, preparation for the quickly approaching anniversary celebration providing the perfect excuse. She'd crisscrossed the town and made the hour-long trip to New Orleans twice this week, making sure her errand running didn't start until just before the high school let out for the day. But today was Friday, and Corey was off for the rest of the weekend. She knew her time had run out.

She shored up her defenses and headed for the back porch. Corey sat in the chair she'd left unoccupied, snapping the ends off of string beans as if he'd been doing so his entire life. Mya stopped just inside the opened kitchen door and leaned against the doorjamb, marveling at the absurdity of her grandmother and Corey Anderson shooting the breeze like a couple of old friends.

"You've been following the doctor's orders?" he asked Grandma.

"Of course," her grandmother answered. The model patient. Mya managed to suppress her sarcastic snort. "I'm not as hard-headed as Maureen makes me out to be."

"I know you're not." Corey laughed. "And I also know that you're going to do a better job at keeping up with your diet."

"You're starting to sound like the two pests in this house," she said.

"Hey!" Mya pushed away from the door-jamb and walked farther onto the porch. "I resent being called a pest."

"There you are," her grandmother said. "I was wondering what was taking you so long. Now, go right back inside and pack yourself a bag. Somebody is whisking you away for the weekend."

"Excuse me?" Mya looked from her grandmother to Corey.

"Not the entire weekend," he said. "Just overnight."

"*Excuse* me?" she said again. "I can't spend the night with you."

His brow lifted, and Mya's entire body blushed. She turned to her grandmother. "And just what kind of example are you set-ting, urging me to pack a bag?"

"Oh, Mya, you're not children anymore. There's nothing wrong with the two of you going away for the weekend."

Who is this person? Mya was pretty sure she was the same woman who had threatened to call the cops on Corey if he dared to touch her granddaughter.

"We're supposed to can green beans today," Mya said, inwardly cringing at her flimsy excuse.

Corey saw right through it. She was so tempted to slap that smug smile off his lips, but he looked so scrumptious sitting there that she had a hard time doing anything but stare at him.

Her grandmother was no help at all. She flung a nonchalant wave toward Mya. "As if I can't get this done by myself. Go pack your bag. Corey says he has a surprise for you."

"She's right, Peaches. You're going to love it. I promise."

Mya cut him with a narrowed gaze, not trusting him one bit. But she had to admit she was intrigued. Without another word of protest, she turned and went back toward the kitchen door.

"Make sure to include an evening dress," Corey called.

She twisted and eyed him with a curious lift to her brow, but he just continued grinning like the proverbial cat with cream. "I don't have an evening dress," she said.

"Fine, we'll find something at the mall."

"As long as it's not at that outlet mall in

Maplesville," her grandmother said.

"No, we'll need to go a step above an outlet mall," Corey said.

Intrigued beyond belief, Mya hurried to her room and threw clothes and toiletries into the carry-on bag she'd brought from New York. Twenty minutes later, she was ensconced in a soft leather bucket seat, waving goodbye to her grandmother.

"Nice car," Mya said as they backed out of the driveway.

"Thanks," he answered. "One of the few indulgences from my baseball-playing days."

"You don't call a five-thousand-square-foot house for one man an indulgence?" she asked.

"That's an investment," he said. "And there won't always be just one person living there. I still have hopes of filling it with a wife and children."

Mya quelled her runaway heartbeat, but nothing would suppress the almost dream-like image that flashed across her mind's eye. She saw herself and a couple of children that looked unmistakably like Corey playing in that massive backyard.

Mya gave herself a mental shake, forcing a picture of her Brooklyn apartment to the forefront of her mind. But all that did was cause a twinge of claustrophobia to close up her throat. Compared to Corey's spacious home, her apartment was a shoebox.

"Where are we going?" Mya asked as he headed south on Highway 21.

"First, we're going shopping," he said. "We've got to get you a dress for dinner."

"Where are we going for dinner?"

He glanced at her from behind dark sunglasses. "Why don't you just relax and enjoy the ride. I promise you'll like it."

Mya wanted to press him, but knew it would be futile. She settled more comfortably in the soft leather as they cruised along the interstate, across Lake Pontchartrain and into downtown New Orleans.

Once in the city, they made their way to world-famous Canal Street. Corey drove all the way to the base of the long boulevard, where it butted against the Mississippi River. He made a U-turn and pulled up to the valet at The Shops at Canal Place.

"We're shopping *here*?" Mya asked. She and Phylicia had window-shopped in the ultra-high-end stores dozens of times when they were younger, but never had they made a purchase.

"Yes, we are," Corey said. "But quickly. Our dinner reservations are in less than a half hour."

They went to Saks Fifth Avenue and Mya

fell in love with the first cocktail dress she encountered. It was black, strapless and hugged her hips and waist. She walked out of the dressing room and did a slow twirl. She could practically feel the heat in Corey's gaze on her skin.

"I cannot wait to take that off of you," he said.

A mother and teenage daughter searching through a rack of dresses both turned to stare. The girl giggled. The mother did not. Embarrassment washed over Mya's entire being.

"Come on," Corey said. "Let's get out of here."

He paid for the dress, and they exited the store. The valet brought the car around within minutes. Mya grabbed her black heels from her bag and slipped them on.

"I love the way your legs look in those shoes," Corey said. "The day of the funeral, I was amazed that you were able to balance in those high heels. You are so sexy, Mya."

"Only you would be concentrating on a woman's legs at a funeral." She laughed.

"I'm sure I wasn't the only one."

They drove into the French Quarter. He made a right onto Chartres Street, a left on St. Louis and then another quick left onto Royal Street. When he pulled up to the curb at Brennan's Restaurant, Mya actually squealed.

"We're going to Brennan's?" she shrieked.

Corey grinned as he put the car in Park. "I'm about a decade and a half late, but I told you I'd bring you here, didn't I?"

Corey had promised to bring her to the world-famous French Quarter restaurant after her prom. Mya knew he couldn't afford it, so she wasn't disappointed when they'd had to settle for a chain restaurant in nearby Metairie. It was only after prom night that Corey had told her that he did have the money. He'd spent an entire month working evenings and weekends in his dad's auto repair shop, despite how much he loathed it, only to learn that reservations at Brennan's were scooped up months in advance.

"How did you manage to get a reservation on such short notice?" she asked.

"I'm not giving out my secrets," he said as he exited the car.

They were guided to a table for two in the restaurant's courtyard, where old-world gas lamps flickered against the backdrop of lush vegetation. They feasted on some of the most amazing food Mya had ever tasted. She'd dined at some of New York's best restaurants, but there was nothing like New

Orleans cuisine. The succulent crabmeat in a creamy béarnaise sauce melted on her tongue, and the chardonnay it was paired with was simply exquisite.

After their entrée dishes had been cleared away, a member of the waitstaff rolled a small flambé cart to their table and, with the flair of a seasoned performer, prepared the restaurant's signature dessert, Bananas Foster. The creamy butter, brown sugar, rum and banana concoction was poured over vanilla bean ice cream.

Mya slid a spoonful in her mouth and her eyelids closed as a moan escaped her throat. She opened her eyes to find Corey staring at her from across the table, his dessert untouched.

"Aren't you going to try it?"

"I'll have my dessert later," he said.

Her entire body warmed, and it had nothing to do with the heated sauce. Their plates were soon cleared, and Mya was almost embarrassed by the amount of anticipation flowing through her veins. She knew what was coming next. She'd seen it in every one of Corey's smoldering stares.

As they walked out of the restaurant, she stopped at the line for the valet, but Corey tugged her arm. "I'm leaving the car here," he said. "We're not going very far."

He tucked her arm in the crook of his elbow and they started walking on Royal Street.

"Corey, where are we — ?" She stuttered to a stop as she stared ahead at the Hotel Monteleone. "You didn't?" Mya said with an awe-filled sigh.

"I did," he said. Corey leaned over and pressed a kiss to her temple. "A night in the Tennessee Williams Suite awaits you."

Mya's eyes filled with tears and her throat clogged with so much emotion she could hardly catch her breath. He was re-creating one of her biggest fantasies. Ever since their literature class had attended a production of *A Streetcar Named Desire,* Mya had been swept away by the world of Tennessee Williams. How had Corey remembered that?

"Wait." She tugged his arm. "My clothes are in the car."

"No, they're not. I had the valet service at Brennan's deliver them to the hotel concierge. Now, come on. I'm ready to get you into that room and out of that dress."

A shiver of wanting passed through her, and Mya quickly followed him into the hotel. She was struck by the lushly appointed lobby, with its marble floors and extravagant chandeliers. Corey spent less than two minutes checking them in at the front desk. Moments later, they were on the elevator heading to the fourteenth floor.

"I can't believe you did all of this," Mya said.

"I'm trying to make up for my past sins," he said.

Her heart constricted. He wasn't the only one with a long-ago sin.

"Corey," she started, but he stopped her with a finger to her lips. His mouth followed. He pressed a delicate kiss upon her lips and murmured, "Not tonight. Tonight is for you, and I want it to be magical."

They arrived at the fourteenth floor, and he ushered her to their room. *The Tennessee Williams Suite* was etched into a placard next to the door.

Mya didn't have a chance to observe their surroundings. As soon as Corey closed the door behind her, he crushed his mouth to hers and scooped her into his arms. He carried her across the massive parlor and into the bedroom, where he laid her gently onto the bed and swiftly removed her new dress. He stripped out of his clothes and, moments later, stretched his taut, muscled body over hers.

Mya wrapped her arms around his neck and pulled his mouth to hers. She closed her eyes and lost herself in the fantasy he'd created. The boy she'd loved with every drop of her soul had turned into the kind of man a woman would kill for. He took such care as he slowly, skillfully made love to her.

With single-minded intensity, he explored her body, kissing his way along her neck to the valley between her breasts. He trailed his tongue down her rib cage, dipping it into her belly button before focusing on that part of her that craved his attention. Mya panted shallow breaths as he palmed her hips and held her firmly in place. Her breath hitched with every delicious lash of his tongue, until she thought she would pass out from the sheer pleasure his extremely capable mouth wielded.

She came with a blinding rush of light sparking behind her closed eyelids. Before she could catch her breath, Corey pushed her knees farther apart and entered her in one smooth thrust.

Mya's back bowed off the bed.

"Just relax," Corey whispered in her ear. Gripping her backside in his hands, he nestled his lips in the crook between her shoulder and her neck and began stroking with a languorous rhythm that turned Mya's body into a relaxed pile of useless muscle. He did all of the work, leaving her there to just enjoy the journey.

Mya felt the beginnings of another orgasm stir deep in her belly. As if he sensed it, Corey's thrusts came harder, faster. He hooked his arms underneath her knees and tilted her legs forward, creating an angle that allowed him to go deeper than ever before.

The orgasm hit with amazing speed, rushing through her body to every extremity.

Seconds later, Corey's body tensed above her and he came in a shattering climax. He collapsed on top of her, his sweat-slicked chest crushing her breasts. Corey quickly rolled to the side and scooped her up against him.

"Damn, that was good," he whispered against her temple.

"You get no complaints from me," Mya said, pulling his arm more securely around her. She nestled against him, stroking his arm. "Thank you, Corey. Really, this was amazing."

"Which part?" he asked.

"Every part. All of it. The fact that you even remembered how much I've always wanted to dine at Brennan's. How much I wanted to stay here, in this very suite."

"I remember everything about you, Mya. I told you once before, you're not the kind of woman a man forgets. Even at seventeen, you were remarkable."

He tried to move her hand away, but Mya tightened her hold on his arm. She wasn't ready to let go of him yet.

"Where are you trying to go?" she asked.

"I have something for you. I'll only be a minute."

"Can't it wait?"

"Yes, but I don't want to." He pressed a kiss to the top of her head. "I'll be right back."

As he headed for the separate parlor, Mya snuggled among the pillows in the king-size bed, finally registering the opulence surrounding her. The thick drapery and plush carpeting made the suite everything she'd always known it would be. She still could not believe the trouble Corey had gone to in order to create such a majestic night, especially after she'd left him in bed last Sunday morning.

Her brave attempt not to fall in love with him again was facing its biggest challenge at this very moment. What woman could guard her heart against such a skilled, well-thought-out seduction?

Corey came back into the room. It took Mya a moment to notice the small gift bag he carried in his right hand; her attention was focused solely on his extremely fit, extremely naked body. He settled back against the headboard, pulling a sheet over his lap.

"Modest?" she asked.

"I don't want anything distracting you from your gift," he returned.

She rolled her eyes as he held the silver gift bag out to her. Mya reached inside and pulled out a square box the size of her palm. When she lifted the lid, the air in her lungs evaporated. Every thought in her mind escaped. Every emotion in her entire being congealed into a ball of unrivaled disbelief as she stared at the fleur-de-lis charm set in shimmering emeralds and sapphires.

"Oh, my God," Mya breathed. Instant tears sprung in her eyes. "Corey? How did you? When?" She looked up at him, but her watery vision obscured his face. "How did you find it?" she asked.

"Magic," he said.

"Corey, I'm serious. I thought you said Elvin Armant sold everything in the antiques shop?"

"Don't worry about how I got my hands on it. Just know that it now belongs to you. Forever." He cradled her cheek in his palm and pressed his lips against her mouth with intoxicating sweetness. "So do I, Mya. You've owned my heart for so long, I can't imagine it in the hands of anyone else. It's all yours."

Mya couldn't utter a single word. But then she didn't have to. With knowledge of her body only he possessed, Corey lowered her back onto the bed and coaxed every drop of emotion from her as he made love to her long into the night.

CHAPTER 11

Corey heard the ringing, but he was too weak to move a solitary muscle. He lifted his head and eyed his cell phone vibrating just a few feet away on the ornate credenza.

"Are you going to answer that?" Mya's husky voice was muffled by the pillow.

"No." He twisted around and pulled her against him, his body stirring to life in anticipation of what he planned to do with her this morning.

The phone started ringing again.

Corey growled as he pushed himself up from the bed. Stark naked, he padded over to the dresser and grabbed the phone.

"Hello?" he snapped. "Andre?" Anxiety tightened his stomach. "What's wrong? Where are you?"

Corey tried to concentrate on the boy's muffled words. A minute later, he hung up the phone and turned to Mya. She'd sat up in the bed, her eyes wide with concern.

"Is everything okay?" she asked.

"No," Corey said, trying to ignore the pull in his belly at the sight of her bare shoulders, knowing how naked she was underneath the silken sheet she'd tucked under her arms. "That was one of my baseball players, Andre Thomas."

"Brandy's son. You told me about him. What's wrong?"

"He's stuck out in the middle of nowhere, at an abandoned warehouse on Highway 190 somewhere past Covington. Said his cousin T.J. asked him to help with a job. Turned out to be something illegal. Andre wouldn't tell me what, though. He doesn't want to get his cousin in trouble."

Corey reached for the overnight bag he'd set on the credenza and pulled out a T-shirt. "I guess I should be happy he backed out of whatever the hell T.J. is mixed up in, but I'm still pissed at him for following his cousin out there in the first place. I told him to stay away from that boy."

According to the rumors he'd heard around town, T.J. had supplied the drugs Andre's mother had been caught peddling. Like Corey's own brothers had been for him, T.J. was the worst kind of influence for a boy Andre's age.

Mya slid out of bed and started dressing.

With each stitch of clothing she put on Corey silently cursed Andre's bad timing. This was *not* how he'd expected their romantic getaway to end.

"I'm sorry about this," he told Mya. "I'll drive you back to your grandmother's and then see about picking up Andre."

"But if he's past Covington, doesn't it make more sense to just take the Causeway bridge from here? It'll cut your drive time in half."

"I'm not dragging you with me."

"Be real, Corey. That boy doesn't need to stay out there any longer than he has to. I'm coming with you," Mya said in a tone that brooked no further argument.

Corey walked the couple of blocks to get his car while Mya finished getting dressed. By the time he'd squared away the bill with the front desk she had made it to the lobby. Once in the car, they headed west on I-10 toward the Causeway bridge in Metairie, just outside of the New Orleans city limits.

Corey filled Mya in on some of the run-ins he'd had with Andre over the past year. Stupid, petty incidents that would stop a major Division One school from adding Andre to their roster, despite his talent on the baseball diamond.

Once they crossed Lake Pontchartrain and

started west on Highway 190, Corey called Andre to get a better idea of where the boy thought the warehouse was located. Fifteen minutes later, Corey spotted the abandoned corrugated steel building. He turned off the highway and started down a short drive riddled with potholes. He caught sight of Andre standing underneath a covered entryway.

Corey tightened his hands on the steering wheel, trying like hell to calm himself down before he did something he'd regret.

Mya put a hand on his forearm. "Hear him out," she said.

Corey nodded. Taking a deep breath, he got out of the car and started toward Andre, with Mya following a few feet behind him.

"Thanks for coming, Coach," Andre mumbled as Corey approached.

"Don't thank me yet. I haven't decided if I'm going to take you home or leave your ass out here. What the hell were you thinking, Andre?"

The boy didn't say anything, just looked down at the ground.

Corey leaned in close and aimed a finger at the boy's chest.

"The problem is you just don't realize how good you've had it. I should have kicked you off the team after you and those

230

other knuckleheads trashed Donaldson's house, but I let it slide. Then I catch you stealing beer, and I let *that* slide. But I told you to stop following behind that cousin of yours. Now, tell me why in the hell I should give you any more chances?"

Andre remained stubbornly silent, and Corey saw red, especially when he thought about what he *could* be doing right now with Mya back in their hotel suite.

"Answer me!" he roared. "Why are you still hanging out with T.J. when I told you to stay away from him?"

"Because nobody else cares," Andre shouted. His hands fisted at his sides as he stared defiantly at Corey. "T.J. is the only one who gives a crap about me. My mama doesn't want me going to see her in jail. I try to talk to Aunt Kendra, but she acts like she can't even see me. None of them care about me."

Corey's anger instantly abated the minute the tears started to flow down Andre's cheeks.

"Dammit," he whispered as he grabbed the boy by the shoulder and brought him into his embrace.

"T.J. is the . . . only one . . . I've got," Andre blubbered.

"No, he's not," Corey said, patting Andre's

back. He pulled him away in order to look him in the eyes. He had to get through to the boy before Andre found himself in the same situation his mother was in.

"I know it's hard not having your mom around, but you need to realize that T.J. doesn't care about you as much as you may think he does. He's using you, Andre. What happened today should show you that. And your Aunt Kendra." Corey shook his head. "Look, I've known her since we were kids, and she's always been selfish. To tell you the truth, I was surprised when I learned that she'd agreed to take you in."

He captured Andre's shoulders and gave them a squeeze. "But you do have people who care about you," Corey emphasized. "It keeps me up at night, trying to figure out how to get through to you and show you that I care about you. I care about all of you on the team. You're like the sons I never had, and my main goal as a coach is to see that you all succeed. Not just on the baseball diamond, but in life. Do you understand, Andre?"

The boy nodded and sniffed, his body jerking with barely reined-in sobs.

Corey brought him in for another hug. He looked over Andre's head and spotted Mya. Her face, like Andre's, was saturated with tears. Before he could ask if she was okay, she spun around and raced toward the other side of the building.

Mya ran like the hounds of hell were snapping at her heels. She collapsed against the side of the rusty corrugated building, using her arm to muffle cries that quickly turned to sobs.

For years she'd wondered what type of father Corey would have been to her baby if she had not miscarried. It was unrealistic to compare the seventeen-year-old high school senior who had gotten her pregnant to the man she'd just seen comforting Andre. But witnessing his compassion and the tough, yet understanding, way he'd handled the troubled teen touched the very depths of her soul.

Seconds later, Corey came around the building and stooped next to her. "What happened? Are you okay?"

"I'm fine," Mya choked out, and pointed at her throat. "Something went down the wrong way," she lied.

"Do you need some water? I may have a bottle in the car." His voice still brimmed with compassion, this time for her. It only helped in pushing Mya even closer to the edge. The tidal wave of emotion was so unexpected she could barely contain it.

For years she'd done all she could not to dwell on the baby she'd lost. Every so often she would see a young mother pushing a stroller and feel overwhelmed with sadness. She would quickly remind herself that she'd dodged a bullet with that long-ago miscarriage and the sadness would be replaced with gratefulness.

But for the first time, Mya allowed herself to imagine what might have been. She closed her eyes and pictured that baby with Corey's eyes and her curly hair. She saw Corey sitting up in bed, reading fairy tales at bedtime, the way her grandfather used to read to her.

A sense of wanting, like nothing she'd ever experienced before, crashed into her. She wanted what she'd lost. The baby. The life with Corey. She wanted it all.

Corey smoothed his hand down her back. "Mya, what's wrong? Talk to me." The concern in his voice prompted another bout of sobs, but she quelled them, pulling in several deep breaths.

"I'm fine. Really." She pressed the heels of her hands into her eyes. "Sorry about that."

Corey gazed at her with a wary frown. "Give me a minute," he said before taking off. He returned moments later carrying a half-full bottle of water. "It's a little warm," he said, handing the bottle to her.

"Thank you." She took a sip of water and nodded toward Andre. "Is he okay?"

Corey propped his hands on his hips and shook his head. "Not really. I'm going to need to talk to Aunt Kendra."

"I'll bet you're looking forward to that," Mya choked out with a laugh, but Corey didn't share her humor. He was staring at her again with that intense gaze that seemed to look straight into her soul. "I'm fine," she told him. "Please stop looking at me like that. We're here for Andre. Let's make sure he's okay."

"Don't think for a minute that I'm just going to let this drop, Mya. You know me better than that."

She did. Which was why she was going to try her hardest to stave off his questions until after the anniversary celebration, when she would no longer be here to answer them.

Because despite how much she wanted it, Mya knew it was too late for a life with Corey. Their worlds were too different, their history together too much to overcome.

But there was one thing in their past that could not remain there. She'd kept it buried too long. And after what she'd witnessed today, she had no choice.

Before she went back to New York, Mya knew she had to tell Corey about the baby.

Corey adjusted his back in an attempt to dislodge the tree bark that was digging into his flesh. He stared at the sexy curve of Mya's spine as she stood hunched over, a fishing rod clutched in her hands. Her concentration was zeroed in on the murky pond. Corey bit back a laugh. She'd tried her hardest to become a city girl, but small-town living was ingrained in her. This was where she belonged. In this town. With him.

She would refute it; Corey knew her well enough to predict her reaction. But there was no denying what was going on here. Last Saturday had been about more than just falling into bed again, it had been about falling back in love.

Though, if he were being honest, Corey could admit that he'd never stopped loving her, despite the years they had been apart. Their love had been young, but it had been real. And in fifteen years Corey had never succeeded in finding a woman who could hold a candle to Mya. He'd tried, but no one had even come close.

He was done searching. He had Mya back. He wasn't letting her go.

"Why haven't you ever married?" Corey asked her. She looked at him, her eyes wide as she stared at him in mute shock.

He tilted his head to the side. "Why?" he asked again.

She returned her attention to the water and recast her fishing rod into the pond. "I'm guessing 'I just never got around to it' won't fly with you, will it?" she asked.

"No," Corey answered. He pushed up from his relaxed position and sat next to her at the pond's edge. Slipping his arms around her waist, he rested his chin on her shoulder, inhaling her unique scent that the swampy water could not mask. "After all these years, Mya, why didn't you ever get married?"

He felt the deep sigh that rumbled through her body.

"You were hard to replace," she finally answered. Her softly spoken admission was so profound Corey could hardly breathe. "To be honest, I never even came close," Mya continued. "I thought this one guy, Derrick, could possibly turn into something meaningful. We were together for nearly two years, but the connection just wasn't there, you know?"

He knew exactly what she was talking about. His longest relationship had lasted just over a year.

Corey reached forward and pulled the fishing rod from her fingers. He tossed it to the ground before gripping Mya's wrists and turning her to face him. He brought his hands up to her shoulders and massaged them.

"What else?" he asked. He would get her to admit she still loved him.

"What?" She sighed. "What more do you want me to say, Corey? That no man has ever lived up to you? I just admitted that." She shook her head, expelling a mirthless laugh as she lifted her eyes to his. "It was always so easy with you. We never had to work at finding things to say to each other. We were always so comfortable together. That's what was missing with the others. I've only had that with you."

As he stared into her lovely face, Corey knew he was done. Completely, undeniably done. He'd never find another woman better suited for him than the one before him. They'd lost fifteen years, but they wouldn't lose any more. They were meant to be together. It was as simple as that.

"Stay," he said.

Mya's head jerked back. "What?"

"Don't go back to New York."

She stared at him, her mouth gaped open.

238

"I have to," she said. "My life is in New York. My work is there. My apartment. Everything. It's my home."

"*This* is your home." Corey tightened his grip on her shoulders. "Deny it all you want, but this place is in your blood. You care about what happens to Gauthier. If you didn't, you would have left the minute your grandmother got out of the hospital. It's your home, Mya. It's time for you to come back to it."

She shook her head. "No," she choked out. "When I left Gauthier it was for good, Corey. I'm going to visit more often — I've already decided that. But my life is no longer here."

She wrangled out of his hold and picked up her fishing rod. Turning back to the pond, she cast her line into the water, her back rigid, her head defiantly upright. Corey reached out for her, but pulled his hand back before making contact.

There were so many things he could argue, so much more he wanted to say, but he sensed her resolve. She was as stubborn as she was beautiful, but if she thought this was the end of this conversation, she was out of her mind.

He wasn't done with Mya. Not by a long shot.

CHAPTER 12

The salty aroma of fried chicken wafting through the air caused Mya's stomach to automatically react, growling like a tiger despite the fact that she'd eaten some of her grandmother's panfried shortcake with warm syrup just two hours ago — a late afternoon snack. It should be a sin to eat like this. Oh, wait, it was. Gluttony definitely described her eating habits over the past three and a half weeks.

"Mya, can you check on the corn bread while you're in there?" her grandmother called.

Mya returned the pitcher of sweet tea to the refrigerator and, donning an oven mitt, pulled the oven's top rack out. The golden-brown corn bread set her mouth to water, and Mya mentally tacked on another mile to her evening run.

"It's done," she shouted toward the dining room where her grandmother had spent the past three days making green-and-white "Celebrate Gauthier" lapel ribbons for this coming weekend's celebration. Mya stopped just inside the doorway. The table was littered with hot glue sticks, ribbon scraps and God knew what else.

"I'm heading down to Main Street to see how things are coming along," she told her grandmother. "The electrician I hired to get the waterwheel back up and running should be there in about twenty minutes."

"I sure hope he can get it working by Saturday."

"So do I," Mya said. "It wouldn't be Heritage Park without the wheel. I'll pick up some non-fat frozen yogurt to go with the peach pie on my way back." Her grandmother grimaced, but Mya completely ignored it. Grandma was lucky both Mya and Aunt Mo had made concessions on most of the food she was preparing for tonight's dinner. The civic association was meeting one last time to finalize everything for Saturday. It had been Mya's idea to have a dinner as a thank-you for all their hard work.

She grabbed Aunt Mo's keys and left through the kitchen door. As she made her way down Pecan Drive she pulled her cell phone from her purse. She needed to touch base with the carnival company that was providing the cotton candy machine on Saturday.

Before she could dial, her cell phone started to vibrate. Mya recognized the 212 area code, but not the New York number.

"Hello," she answered.

"Mya?"

"Ricki?" she asked, identifying her colleague's voice. She'd worked with Ricki Stanzi on a number of shows.

"Yeah, it's me. I'm happy I finally got you. I've tried a couple of times."

"Sorry about that. Cell phone coverage here is spotty at times. What's up?"

"Are you sitting down?" Ricki asked.

Mya rolled her eyes at the woman's dramatics. "Technically," she answered.

"The new buzz going around the circuit is that *Hitsville* secured the funding it needed. It looks like it's a go."

Mya stomped harder on the brake at the stop sign than was necessary. "How sure are you?" she asked.

"About ninety percent. You know how these things work," Ricki said. "Investors have been known to pull out at the last minute, but it sounds as if the group taking on *Hitsville* is pretty solid."

"You know how much I'd love to work on

that show," Mya said. *Hitsville* was based on the early days of Motown Records. As soon as she'd heard about it, Mya had started thinking up costuming ideas from that era. "Is there any talk about when they plan to start preproduction?"

"Not yet, but I'll keep my ears open. You need to get yourself back here," Ricki said. "You don't want to miss this opportunity."

No, she didn't. Mya already had a solid reputation in the theater community, known as one of the go-to costume designers. Her Tony Award nomination had boosted her career significantly, but if she could pull off the ideas she had for *Hitsville,* her career would skyrocket.

She could not pass up the chance to work on this show. This is what she lived for, what she'd spent the past decade building and nurturing.

It was time for her to head back home.

As Mya drove along Main Street, a heavy cloud settled over her heart. She looked from side to side, pride tightening her chest at the thought of the role she'd played in helping to spruce up the street. But sorrow and regret lodged in Mya's throat.

This was home, too. She'd spent fifteen years pushing Gauthier out of her life, and in just a few weeks the town had wormed its way back into her heart. At odd moments, when she'd let her guard down, she'd pictured life here, tucked away in this sleepy little town. She could see it all too well. Enjoying Sunday dinner at her grandmother's, cheering on Corey's baseball team in the stands at the high school games, cuddling up to him every night in that huge bed.

God, she wanted that. But she couldn't do it.

New York was easier. She had a successful career and the freedom to travel and see the world.

Staying in Gauthier would be the opposite of easy. It would be catastrophic. These past few weeks had been a mirage — an illusion of what life could have been if she didn't know better. But she *did* know better. Reality was only steps away from her, working behind the counter of the Gauthier Pharmacy and Feed Store. She'd escaped the snares of this town once. She wasn't going to put herself in a position to get caught again, no matter how much joy she'd experienced these past few weeks with Corey.

He was the biggest threat of all. Just as he'd done fifteen years ago, Corey Anderson had her considering giving up her dreams — giving up the life she'd built for herself.

She would not allow anyone to do that.

"Just get through Saturday and get back to New York," Mya told herself.

It was time for her to get back to her old life.

By the time she arrived back at her grandmother's, the yard was crowded with cars. The meeting wasn't officially supposed to start for another half hour, but when the majority of the committee was made up of retirees who no longer lived by a watch, start times didn't mean all that much.

As she alighted from the car, Mya spotted Corey's SUV coming down the street. He pulled up alongside the fence and got out.

It had been three days since she'd seen him. She'd dodged his calls and managed to miss him the two times he'd stopped in at Grandma's.

"Hi," she said as he walked up to her.

The intense look on his face told her that he saw straight through her innocent greeting.

"We graduated from high school years ago, Mya. I'm not playing games as if we're still teenagers." Corey stepped forward and took each of her hands in his. His stare brooked no room for pretense.

"I love you," he said. "I've loved you most of my life and I want to build a life with you. And I know you love me, too, Mya. I'm willing to do whatever it takes to make this work, but you have to be willing, too. The ball is in your court."

He leaned forward and pressed an innocent kiss to her forehead.

"I'm on my way to speak with the developers and convince them that they no longer want to build their new store in Gauthier. Give my regards to the rest of the committee." He gave her another kiss, then turned and headed back for his truck.

Mya stood in the middle of the yard, completely stunned.

How had this happened?

When she'd boarded the plane to return home for her grandfather's funeral less than a month ago, she could not have fathomed the twists and turns her life — and heart — would take. How had she found herself back here, in love with Corey?

Mya stood rooted in that spot until Aunt Mo came outside looking for her a solid five minutes later. She lied to her aunt, telling her she had a couple of things to get from the car. Mya used the short reprieve to compose herself.

She could take the easy way out and run back to New York. It would be the simplest answer. She could pick up her life right where it had left off before her grandfather's death.

Maybe running made her a coward. Maybe it made her no better than her mother — the queen of running. But it would also make her smart.

The other choice was one that made her breath hitch and her blood run cold. She could stay in Gauthier and face the fears that had kept her away for so many years: the fear of becoming trapped in this small town, of losing the opportunity to really live.

The fear of revealing the truth to Corey about the child she'd lost.

She needed to face it — face *him.* She'd used the miscarriage as an impetus to run years ago. She couldn't cower to her fears any longer.

Despite the anxiety chilling her blood at the thought of finally sharing the truth about her pregnancy, Mya knew it had to be done.

His muscles shook, weariness making them tired and weak, but Corey went for another board of plywood anyway. The pain in his legs and shoulders kept his focus on something other than Mya. At least that had been his plan when he'd pulled into Jamal's driveway and offered his services.

He squinted to keep the droplet of sweat from entering his eye, pulling out nails he held between his lips and hammering the board in place. Once relieved of his burden, he wiped his brow and reached for the beer Jamal had brought him a couple of minutes ago.

"Hey, man," his friend said, nodding toward the sheets of plywood Corey had hung. "I appreciate the hard work, but you're going to wear yourself out if you don't ease up."

"I didn't come here to ease up," Corey said. He set the beer on the floor and went for another sheet of plywood. Jamal grabbed the other end and held it in place while Corey pounded nails with more force than necessary.

Jamal looked over at him with a big, stupid grin on his face.

"What's so funny?" Corey asked.

Jamal shook his head. "Sexual frustration is a bitch. Am I right?"

Corey let out a derisive snort.

"Hey, I've been there, man," his friend said. "Why do you think I spend so much time working on this damn house? Manual labor is a poor substitute, though."

"If it's that bad, why don't you get laid? I can name at least twenty women in this town who would line up for the opportunity."

"A quick lay doesn't have the same appeal it had when I was in my twenties," Jamal said. "Besides, I could say the same for you. Though I don't think you'd jump at the chance to get with just any willing woman, either. How long have you had it bad for Mya Dubois?"

"High school," Corey answered, because what was the use in denying it? All Jamal had to do was ask anyone in town.

"Is she thinking of staying in Gauthier?" his friend asked.

"I don't think so," Corey answered after a pause. The words were harder to voice than he'd thought they would be. But he hadn't heard from Mya since he'd caught her outside of her grandmother's house before the celebration dinner. He'd started dialing her number three times over the past twenty-four hours, but had stopped midway each time.

He'd laid his heart bare. The decision was hers to make.

Corey feared she'd already made it.

She would be gone in two days. He felt it in his bones, and the ache that came with this inevitable truth ripped through his body. Mya had crushed him once before. It had taken him years to get over it. This time, Corey knew it would take even longer to recover.

It would take a lifetime.

CHAPTER 13

The sun shone like a beacon, smiling down on the town of Gauthier. The weather report called for crystal-blue skies, low humidity and temperatures in the low eighties. Mya considered the perfect weather a gift from God. He knew how important today was for the town.

The downtown area was decked out for the celebration. Food booths lined the street, with locals selling everything from homemade jams and jellies to one of her personal favorites, crawfish pie. Green-and-white streamers draped from light pole to light pole, and a huge banner stretched across the entrance to Main Street, held up on either side by ladders extended from the Gauthier and Maplesville fire trucks.

Mya moved the basket of lapel ribbons her grandmother had made to the opposite end of the welcome table where people could pick them up after they had browsed the paraphernalia that had been spread across the table. There were registration forms for residents to join the civic association, surveys on how to improve life in Gauthier and pamphlets about the town's history.

"Hey, you," Phil said, giving her a hug. "You need to get to the stage. Mayor Johnson is about to begin the opening ceremony. You should be up there with him."

"I'm not getting onstage, but I do want to hear the announcement," Mya said, following Phylicia. Included in the mayor's opening remarks would be word of Gauthier's connection to the Underground Railroad. They had managed to keep the new findings under wraps, and Mya was anxious to see how the townspeople reacted to the news.

It was more satisfying than she had anticipated. Excitement hummed through the air as folks chatted about the history that had been hidden in plain sight here in Gauthier.

"Pretty sweet." Phil looked over at her. "You're way more gracious than I am, Mya Dubois. If it were me, I'd have hired a skywriter to spell it out overhead. 'It was me! I found the proof!' "

Mya burst out laughing. "I wouldn't say I found the proof, just a few initial cues." And she didn't deserve all the credit. Corey had been there with her. He had earned just as much praise as she had.

She returned to the welcome booth to greet newcomers.

"Honey, this place looks fabulous!" Claudette said.

Mya thanked her as she handed her one of the "Get to Know Main Street" maps that pointed out the businesses and things to do in downtown Gauthier.

"I can't take the credit," she reiterated. "So many people pitched in." She looked around at the crowds, which had swelled in the past couple of hours since she'd arrived. "People seem to be having a good time, though. This should provide a nice boost to the local economy."

"It already has. I've seen more foot traffic in front of my shop this week than I've seen in the past month. You had better take credit for it. A lot of this was your idea."

Claudette motioned for her to come closer. In a loud whisper, she said, "I've heard rumors that those developers are now thinking of bringing their store to Bogalusa instead of Gauthier. They said the town isn't the right market." Claudette squeezed her shoulder. "I think it's because of what you helped to uncover about Gauthier. You did your grandmother proud, Mya. You did us all proud."

The instant lump that formed in Mya's throat nearly choked her.

"Thank you." She ducked her head, discreetly swiping at the tears that gathered at the corner of her eye. "I need to check in on Grandma," she told Claudette. "You mind taking over for a little while?"

Mya handed over greeter duties to Claudette and headed in the direction of the sweets booth where her grandmother and several other ladies from New Hope Baptist Church were selling every homemade dessert imaginable. Different community organizations had purchased the right to sell items. The Knights of Columbus were grilling burgers and hot dogs, the Masons were selling fried seafood and the Gauthier High School Glee Club was making a killing with their snowballs.

Mya kept her eyes averted from the game booths, which were all being manned by members of the high school baseball and track teams. She knew she would have to face Corey sooner or later — in less than an hour, in fact, when the visitors from the local parish tourism board were set to arrive — but she would put it off for as long as possible.

He'd expect an answer to the offer he'd proposed, and she wasn't ready to give him one.

She'd stayed awake half the night, running the list of pros and cons in her head, trying to picture what life would be like if she were to remain in Gauthier. The picture was different than the one she'd seen years ago, as a teenager hell-bent on getting out of this place. Now she was older, wiser. She had more resources at her disposal and could hop on a plane whenever she felt the need to get away. Small-town life no longer resembled a prison sentence.

But her life was in New York. Her work, her friends. Everything she'd worked hard for these past fifteen years. Could she just give it all up?

Maybe she didn't have to give up anything. She could divide her time between both cities, finding sanctuary in Gauthier's peace and quiet when the frenetic pace of the city got to be too much. Heading to New York to work or when Gauthier's calmness had her climbing the walls.

Could she make it work?

Mya had hoped if she asked the question enough, the answer would reveal itself. But she'd asked herself over and over and was still as confused as ever. The only thing she knew for certain was that she had a flight to JFK booked for one o'clock tomorrow afternoon.

Mya dipped under the wooden beam sectioning off the various food booths.

"How's it going?" she asked her grandmother, who was counting dollar bills like a loan shark raking in the night's bounty.

"I don't think I made enough coconut pies," Grandma answered. "It's not even noon yet, and we've sold almost all of them."

"I told you people were going to buy those up," Mya taunted. "You know no one can resist your coconut pies."

"She's right about that."

Mya stiffened at the deep voice only steps away. She turned and wanted to scream at how good Corey looked.

"Good morning, ladies." He addressed all the women in the booth, but even with the sunglasses covering his eyes Mya knew he was looking directly at her.

"Do your players have everything they need?" she asked him. "I have more prizes at Grandma's if they start to run out."

"The only one in danger of running out of prizes is the dunk tank, but I think the opportunity to dunk Assistant Principal Donaldson is enough of a prize for anyone.

Manny's spent about fifty bucks already. Is everything in place for the tourism board?" Corey asked, handing her grandmother a dollar before picking up an oatmeal cookie.

Mya knew better than to be fooled by his easygoing demeanor. "I was going to run over to Matthew Gauthier's office just to make sure Carmen doesn't need any help," she answered.

"I'll come with you," he said, just as she knew he would.

As Mya was leaving the booth, her grandmother grabbed her hand. She looked back, and Grandma sent her a wink.

Oh, great.

Who would have thought having her grandmother hate Corey back in high school would be easier than having her like him now?

Mya left the booth and started toward Gauthier's law office. Corey fell in step beside her, breaking off a piece of his oatmeal cookie. He held it out to her. "Want a bite?"

"No, thanks," Mya answered.

He took the shades from his eyes and hooked them in front of his shirt. "So, are we going to talk about why you've been avoiding me, or should we save it for when we have more time? Although I don't know when we'll find more time since I'm pretty sure you're leaving town as soon as you can."

Mya slowed her steps. "Corey, please."

He stopped and encircled her wrist, halting her steps as well. "The decision was yours to make, Mya. If you've made it, at least grant me the courtesy of letting me know what you chose."

She took a fortifying breath before saying, "My flight leaves at one tomorrow afternoon."

Corey's jaw hardened, but he didn't let her go.

"So that's it," he stated.

"You knew this was temporary," she said. "I've been in Gauthier nearly a month longer than I'd originally planned. My life is in New York, Corey. There's a new show in the works that I've wanted to be a part of ever since I heard it was a possibility."

"That's not why you're leaving," he said. "You told me yourself that a lot of the work you do can be handled remotely. Stop skirting the issue, Mya."

She yanked her wrist from his grip and crossed her arms over her chest. "Fine, you tell me why I'm going."

"Because you're scared," he charged. "You're leaving because the thought of loving me scares the hell out of you, the same way it did fifteen years ago."

She shook her head, vehemently denying his claim. "I was never afraid of loving you. You know I loved you, Corey. I never denied that."

"But you left. You left because you thought loving me meant loving this town, and you were always so damn afraid of getting stuck here." He ran an agitated hand down his face. "You criticize your mother for the way she looked down on Gauthier, but you are just like her. You're still letting some crazy notion of being trapped here keep you away." He stepped up to her, his intense eyes searing a path straight to her soul. "What you don't understand is that leaving here doesn't make you better than anyone, Mya. It just makes you a coward."

Every word from his mouth hit her like a blow to the chest. She wanted to lash out at him. She wanted to pummel his chest with her fist for even daring to compare her to Elizabeth Dubois.

There was only one thing that stopped her: the fact that Corey was right.

She *was* running. Not just from Gauthier, but from the secret she'd been hiding all these years. The truth stabbed at her conscience, taunting her. She knew she would never truly be at peace until she finally came clean to Corey about the baby.

"Mya!"

Both she and Corey spun toward the law office, where Carmen stood just inside the doorway. She pointed toward three vehicles that had just pulled into the parking spots in front of the building. It had to be the people from the tourism board.

Corey let out a frustrated curse. "Come on," he said. "It's showtime."

Corey stood in the corner of the cavernous back room in Matthew Gauthier's law office. Earlier in the week, he, along with a dozen of the players on his team, had helped move about a hundred file boxes into a climate-controlled storage unit in Maplesville. The Washington Parish Historical Society had toured the room on Wednesday, along with a professor from Tulane University's history department, who had quickly determined that this was indeed a stop on the Underground Railroad. The professor was in the middle of a big research project on the Underground Railroad in Louisiana and had set up residence in Matthew's office.

The historical society had asked that the room be closed off to visitors — even to

Matthew and his staff — while they awaited confirmation from the state preservation board, but Mya had explained that an exception would have to be made for representatives from the Louisiana tourism bureau. The pitch was in full swing, and the tourism board seemed to be eating it up.

One by one, they ducked into the opening in the wall that had been discovered once the boxes had been removed. The dank crawl space was illuminated by a low-wattage lightbulb on a tripod. The researchers with the historical society had cautioned against using bright lights that may cause damage to anything that was found.

"This is awe inspiring," one of the representatives said. She held out an arm. "I have goose bumps."

The history professor explained that small, secret rooms such as this one were common back then. He pointed out hash marks on the bricks as markings the slaves used to count down the days until the next push to the North would be made.

They moved from the law office to the other buildings on Main Street. Mya played tour guide, and the irony wasn't lost on Corey. He could hardly stomach hearing her expound on all the wonderful attributes of Gauthier when she was itching to leave the town as soon as possible. How she didn't manage to choke on the words was a miracle.

"Hey, Coach!"

He turned and spotted Pierre Jones jogging toward him. Corey stepped away from the touring contingent. "What's up?" he asked the boy when he arrived.

"It's Andre," Pierre said. "He's talking crazy."

"What do you mean by crazy?" Corey asked, anxiety instantly raising the hair on his neck.

"He says he's leaving. He's got two suitcases and his drum set packed in the back of his truck."

"Dammit," Corey cursed. "Where is he?"

Pierre motioned for him to follow and they took off toward the west end of Main Street. When they turned down Maurepas Drive Corey spotted Andre's dusty gray pickup, with its orange door and red tailgate. The mishmash of truck parts was courtesy of Corey's father's old junkyard.

The boy was sitting behind the wheel when he approached. Corey rapped his knuckle against the glass. Andre's eyes remained straight ahead.

"He told me not to tell anybody," Pierre said from a few feet away. "He sent me to get his iPod from his girlfriend. He wasn't even going to tell her that he was leaving."

"Go on." Corey gestured for Pierre to leave. "I'll take care of this."

Pierre looked at him as if he wasn't sure he should leave Corey alone with a pack of rabid dogs, let alone his best friend, but he nodded and started back toward the festivities.

Corey went around the front of the truck and opened the side door, which he remembered from the team's constant locker room ribbing of Andre, didn't lock. He slid onto the seat, closed the door and stared straight ahead.

"So, you want to talk about this?" he asked Andre.

Andre cursed. Harshly. As an authority figure Corey should have chastised him for it, but it was obvious the boy's problems warranted it.

"I'm going to kill Pierre," Andre said.

Corey hitched a thumb toward the truck bed, which apparently contained all of the kid's belongings. "Where do you think you're going?"

"I don't know," Andre said. "Anywhere but here."

"And what's so wrong with here?" Corey asked.

"No one wants me here."

"Did you and Kendra get into a fight or something? Did she tell you that she doesn't want you here? Is that what you're saying?"

"Kendra don't give a damn about me. And now T.J. don't want nothing to do with me either after I wouldn't deliver that package to that guy for him." Andre hunched his shoulders. He sniffed and wiped at his face. "Don't make sense for me to be here."

"You need to stay the hell away from T.J. anyway," Corey reminded him. "And I know your aunt Kendra isn't the most attentive person in the world, but you'll be out of her house soon enough."

"She already kicked me out of her house," Andre said.

"She what?" Corey twisted in the seat to face him.

"She does it all the time," Andre continued. "If she brings a man home, she makes me leave. I can't just go to my room and shut the door — I have to leave the house. I used to hang out at T.J.'s when she made me leave, but now he won't let me come to his place."

Corey brought his hand up and massaged the tight muscles in the back of his neck. Expelling a tired sigh, he said, "You're coming home with me."

Andre sniffed loudly and looked over at him.

Corey nodded. "I'm not letting you leave Gauthier. I don't know what would have to happen legally, but you're almost eighteen anyway."

"In two months," Andre interjected.

"And once you graduate in May, you're going to college." He clamped a hand on Andre's shoulder. "Everything is going to be okay."

"What about Kendra?" Andre asked.

"Don't worry about your aunt. I'll take care of her," Corey said. He opened the door and slid out of the truck. Before closing it, he reached into his pocket and pulled out his key ring. He unwound his house key from the ring and handed it to Andre. "Go and put your things at my place, then get back here and enjoy the celebration."

Corey closed the door and headed back toward the center of Main Street, his mind on one thing. He spotted Kendra Thomas walking toward the food booths.

"Kendra," he called. "I need to speak with you. Now," he said.

She turned, a coy smile tipping up her lips. "Hi, Corey," she said, running her fingers along his arm.

Corey jerked away from her caress. He

had been turning down Kendra's advances for the past twenty years, ever since she first asked him to the homecoming dance their freshman year of high school. One would think she would have gotten a clue by now.

"Do you know what it means to be a legal guardian?" Corey asked her.

Her smile instantly dimmed. "I don't want to hear anything about Andre," she said. "Andre is fine."

"The hell he is," Corey bit out. "Andre has been getting into trouble left and right, and you act as if you don't see it. You're supposed to be taking care of him."

"I *am* taking care of him," Kendra said. "Andre's not starving. He's not naked. Though God knows he eats like a damn horse and grows out of clothes faster than I can buy them."

"Taking care of someone is more than just buying food and clothes," Corey pointed out. "And you don't put them out of the house when you have 'company' over. Your nephew should come first."

Kendra's pencil-thin eyebrows drew together as a sneer lifted up one corner of her mouth. "Don't you get self-righteous with me, Corey Anderson. I didn't ask for this. I could have let Andre go into the foster care system, but I stepped up and was there for my family. That's more than you can say."

"What the hell are you talking about? I was there for my dad until the day he died. Even when I moved away, I made sure he was taken care of."

"Oh, please. You know I'm not talking about your dad." Kendra rolled her eyes. "Don't act all innocent. I was there when Mya chewed you out after catching you with Tamika Hillard."

Corey winced. He wanted to strangle Kendra for throwing his long-ago mistake in his face. As if it had any bearing on the current situation with her nephew.

"Mr. Stand-up Baseball Star, who turned into a model citizen after years of running the streets with his twin brothers. You wanted to pretend you were so much better than Stefan and Shawn. Yeah, right," Kendra snorted. "Did either of your brothers cheat on their girlfriend after she'd just lost their baby?"

Corey's neck stiffened. "What did you say?" he asked in a soft voice.

Kendra huffed out a cynical laugh. "There's no need to play dumb, Corey. I know all about that baby. You all tried to keep it a secret, but my mama was a nurse at the hospital back then. She took care of Mya the couple of days she was in the hospital after her miscarriage."

Corey's breath caught in his lungs as memories from fifteen years ago assaulted him. He remembered going to visit Mya in the hospital, sitting at her bedside and holding her hand as she recovered from a "stomach virus." He remembered thinking that no stomach virus should be severe enough to put someone in the hospital, but what the hell did he know at the time?

He remembered her crying in his arms and a few weeks later, telling him that she was leaving Gauthier.

A *baby*? Mya had been *pregnant*?

Just the idea of the two of them creating a tiny life together tightened his throat with enough emotion to smother him. How many times over the years had he imagined raising a family with Mya? Dozens? Hundreds? They had been closer to that reality than he'd ever realized, yet he'd had no clue.

Mya had been pregnant with his child and had not bothered to tell him.

No, it was worse than that. Not only had she not bothered to tell him. She'd *lied* about it. For fifteen years she'd been lying to him. How could she have kept something like this from him?

There was only one way to find out.

Anger blurring his sight, Corey spun on

his heel and headed straight for her. He spotted the contingent of tourism officials surrounding the wooden waterwheel in the center of Heritage Park. His eyes quickly zeroed in on his target. She was as animated as a theme park tour guide, pointing out features and smiling at the visitors.

He wondered if that smile would remain when she explained why she'd lied to him for fifteen years.

CHAPTER 14

Mya pointed out the features of the water-wheel, the centerpiece of Heritage Park. She gave the members of the tourism board a brief overview of the history of the wheel and crossed her fingers as she gave Carmen the nod to flip the switch. The waterwheel hesitated for just a second before it jerked to life.

Applause erupted, not only from the tourism board, but from the gathering of Gauthier residents who had congregated a few yards back to watch the big wheel churn after years of being idle. Once the entire park was completely rewired, the wheel would pedal water 24/7.

"If you follow me, we will now visit the Heritage Park gazebo," Mya said. "It dates back to 1867 and was a gift to the town from its founder, Micah Gauthier."

Mya guided the group to the southern edge of the park where the wooden gazebo stood, shaded under the curving branches of centuries-old oak trees. The gazebo was the last stop on the guided tour before she released the tourism board to enjoy the festivities on their own.

As they walked, she searched for Corey in the crowd. He had been gone for nearly a half hour. She wanted Corey by her side when she gave the final pitch for Gauthier to be considered a destination for tourists.

Once they reached the gazebo, Mya pointed out the complex design, with carvings that were so intricate they resembled wooden lace. As the guests studied the workmanship, Mya took the opportunity to scan the crowd once again.

"Finally," she murmured as she spotted Corey striding across the grass toward them. But as he drew closer, Mya's senses went on red alert. Something was wrong. His face was tense with anger, his steps swift and powerful.

Something must have happened with Andre. Mya had no idea what the boy had done to raise Corey's ire, but it must have been really bad.

"This is wonderful," one of the tourism board members remarked.

"The attention to detail is absolutely outstanding," another said.

"Yes, it is, isn't it?" Mya said. She needed to cut this short. From the look on Corey's face, he needed her.

She pasted on another smile for the officials. Taking a deep breath, Mya went in for the kill, reciting the spiel she'd practiced last night. Painting Gauthier as a picture of Southern charm and small-town life, she pleaded with the board to find the town a worthy candidate for marketing Louisiana's rich culture and history to tourists.

Gesturing to the grounds, Mya finished with, "I invite you all to explore everything our town has to offer. Sample the food, get to know the residents. I'm sure you will come to love it as much as everyone in Gauthier does."

Mya shook the hand of each board member, letting out a much-needed sigh of relief as the seven-member group headed toward the festivities on the other end of the park.

"Thank goodness that's over," Mya said.

"You did wonderfully," Carmen said. "They looked very impressed."

"I think so, too." Mya grinned. She turned to Corey, who had stopped just to the right of the gazebo steps. "I could have used a little help from you," she said. "Where have you been?"

He stared at her for several long moments

without saying a word, and when he did speak, it was in a voice so soft, so low and deadly, Mya's skin iced.

"Carmen, can you excuse us for a minute?" he asked.

"Sure." Carmen looked from Mya to Corey. "Is everything okay?"

"We're fine," he said.

A bigger lie had never been told. Mya knew him well enough to know that everything was definitely *not* fine.

She waited until Carmen was well out of hearing distance before she asked, "Corey, what's going on with you? Is everything all right with Andre?"

He didn't say anything, just grabbed her by the arm and yanked her down the gazebo's two steps. He marched them behind the structure, past the last of the park benches and into the heavily shaded area of the park that had yet to be cleared by volunteers. It was still thick with dank vegetation and as private as one could get while still in the open park area.

Mya tried to pull away from him, but his grip was tight, biting into her skin.

"Dammit, let me go," she said with a vicious jerk, finally breaking free. "What is the matter with you?" She rubbed her arm where marks from his fingers had already colored her skin.

"You got something you want to tell me?" he asked.

Mya recoiled at the fury in his tone. "Corey, what are you talking about?" she asked, her own rage escalating at his unwarranted attack.

"You know, Mya, I've been teaching high school kids for a few years now. I know how crazy things can get at the end of the year. Everybody is thinking about prom, graduation, leaving for college. I get it. But one would think that being pregnant and having a miscarriage wouldn't just slip your mind."

Mya's entire body stiffened in shock. Panic twisted around her heart, threading through her bloodstream as reality slammed into her.

Her fifteen-year reprieve was over. The secret was out, laid bare before her.

"I mean, come on," Corey continued with false nonchalance. "You were in the hospital for two days. I remember because I spent every free minute sitting next to your bed. You never once thought that maybe I should know you'd just lost my baby, Mya? Or maybe that *stomach virus* had you so sick, you just couldn't think straight. Was that it?"

Her eyelids slid shut as instant tears

streamed down her cheeks. She knew this would eventually come to light, but *she* had wanted to be the one to tell him.

"I was going to tell you," she started.

"When?" he bit out, his mock casualness replaced with stinging fury. "It's been fifteen years. What, was it never the right time? What was it, Mya?"

She held her hands out, pleading. "You don't understand. That baby represented everything I had feared would happen to me, Corey. Look at what happened to Shelly Hunt and Brandy Thomas. They both got pregnant young, and they both got stuck in Gauthier.

"As horrible as it was to lose that baby, it turned out to be a blessing," she said. Corey flinched. A mixture of hurt and anger encompassed his face, but Mya soldiered on. "I wasn't ready to be a mother any more than you were ready to be a father. I wanted more for myself," she stressed. "I wanted more than this town could provide, and when I got pregnant I saw all my dreams slipping away."

"It still doesn't explain why you never told me about the baby," he seethed.

"What could you have done, Corey? You were on your way to Arizona State. If I had had that baby, I would have been the one stuck here to raise it. Or worse, I would have pulled an Elizabeth Dubois and left it here for Grandma or Aunt Maureen to raise. I refused to allow that to happen."

"Well, I guess that miscarriage was pretty convenient." His stare intensified, his brow creasing into a deep V. "Tell me something, Mya, was it really a miscarriage or did you assist in destroying my baby?"

Mya pulled in a swift gasp. "Are you asking me if I had an abortion?"

He shrugged. "It's a valid question, especially after you just admitted that you were happy you lost my baby. How do I know you didn't get rid of it on purpose?"

"I had a miscarriage," she asserted, "and I never said I was happy. Losing that baby was one of the hardest things I've ever gone through."

Mya wrapped her arms around her upper body, fearing if she let go, she would crack into a million pieces.

"Corey, please listen to me. I'm sorry I kept this from you for so long. I was scared back then. I thought if I told you about the baby, you would have insisted on something crazy, like us getting married or some other noble nonsense. You were so hell-bent on doing the right thing so you could prove you were better than your two brothers."

"And the thought of marrying me just scared the hell out of you," he stated.

"We were *seventeen*!" Mya practically screamed. "Of course it scared me. Everything scared me. I wanted out, Corey. And when I found out I was pregnant, I felt trapped. So maybe you're right. Maybe I didn't tell you because I didn't want to be tied to you. Because you were tied to Gauthier. You still are."

"And you still want out," he said. "Like mother, like daughter."

The look in his eyes was deadly enough to kill, pure venom, and leveled squarely at her.

"Corey, don't do this," Mya pleaded.

But he'd already done it. Mya witnessed the moment the shield went up. He'd cut her out.

Out of his life.

Out of his heart.

Without another word, he turned and walked away.

Mya lowered to the moist ground, her knees cushioned by the uncut grass. But nothing could soften the pain that racked her body. She covered her face with her hands and sobbed until her entire being shook with it.

Corey gripped the SUV's steering wheel so tight his fingers cramped in protest. He couldn't decide what pissed him off more, Mya or his own conscience, which had been niggling at him since the moment he walked away from her.

Why in the hell should he be concerned about her feelings? She'd just admitted to being relieved that she'd lost his child — a child she'd never bothered to tell him about.

Corey gripped the wheel even tighter, his knuckles white underneath his skin. If he moved his hands, he was liable to punch his fist through the window. And he sure as hell didn't need a broken window heaped onto the rest of his problems.

Fifteen years. She'd lied to him for fifteen years.

Her excuses weren't worth a damn in his book. She'd been afraid. He'd give her that one. If she had told him about the baby back when they were in high school he would have been scared, too. Terrified. Neither of them had been in the position to become parents back then. But why in the hell didn't she tell him about the baby after she'd miscarried?

She said she was afraid he'd try to do the honorable thing and marry her. Well, what in the hell was so wrong with that? Back then, before he'd had that monumental slip in judgment and cheated on her, Corey had thought they were heading for marriage. He had not contemplated a life without Mya.

But she had been just fine getting on with her life. Without him. Without their baby. The truth bore down on Corey like an avalanche racing down a mountainside, smothering every sympathetic feeling toward Mya in its path.

She saw him as nothing but an anchor, weighing her down, tying her to this place that she'd continuously sought to break free of. It was the reason she'd run from him years ago. It was the reason she was running now.

Corey slammed his fists against the steering wheel, then jerked the keys out of the ignition. He got out of the truck and stalked into his house, slamming the door so hard the window rattled.

He walked into the living room and spotted Andre lounging on the sofa, a handheld gaming system device balanced in his lap. In a few hours the boy had made himself at home. Their new living arrangement was temporary, but being able to keep tabs on

Andre gave Corey peace of mind he was sorely lacking in every other aspect of his life right now.

Andre looked up from the gaming system. "You okay, Coach?"

"I'm perfect," Corey lied. "How does pizza sound for dinner?"

Andre gave him a thumbs-up. Corey went into the kitchen and speed-dialed Gauthier's sole pizza restaurant, amazed at how something as mundane as ordering dinner could help soothe his frayed state of mind. It was the first step in getting on with his life.

If Mya was so anxious to get back to her life, then it was something he'd just have to deal with. She wanted out? Fine. He was letting her go.

CHAPTER 15

Mya stuffed the two remaining bars of lemon verbena soap into her suitcase and zipped it up. She cast a final, lingering look around the room, making sure she wasn't forgetting anything.

"Mya, you're going to miss your flight if you don't hurry up."

"I'm coming, Aunt Mo," she called out. She pulled the carry-on bag's thick strap over one shoulder and wheeled the small suitcase she'd borrowed from Phylicia to pack the clothes she'd purchased for her extended stay in Gauthier. When she walked into the living room, Mya's throat seized at the crestfallen look on her grandmother's face as she sat in Granddad's old chair.

"Don't look at me like that," she pleaded. "I told you I'll be back in a few months."

"What happened with you and Corey?" her grandmother asked, getting right to the heart of it. "You two had been getting along so well. I was so sure he could convince you to stay."

Mya gave her a sad smile. "Corey doesn't want me in Gauthier," she said.

Corey probably never wanted to see her again. She tried to stave off the rush of pain that thought produced, but it was pointless. The crushing ache permeated every corner of her heart.

Her grandmother captured her hand and squeezed it. "What happened between you two, Mya? Why wouldn't Corey want you in Gauthier?"

Sorrow clogged her throat. "There was just too much in our past to overcome."

"But —"

"It's better this way, Grandma," Mya said, cutting off her protest. "Corey and I just were not meant to be." Mya sucked in a lungful of air as she turned to her aunt. "You ready to hit the road?"

"Just waiting on you," Aunt Mo replied.

Mya stooped down and enveloped her grandmother in a hug, clinging to her for dear life. "Stay away from the sweets," she warned. "I expect to see both you and this town thriving when I come back for your birthday in a few months."

"We will be." Her grandmother patted her back. "Go on now. If you're so damned determined to leave, you better get going before you miss your plane."

"Mama, stop that cursing!" Maureen admonished.

Mya choked out a teary laugh. She gave her grandmother one last kiss on the cheek before retrieving her bags and walking through the door Maureen held open for her. She slipped into the passenger seat and fought like mad to keep her tears at bay. It was a valiant fight, but one Mya doubted she'd win. Her throat tightened with every inch of gravel the tires ate up as Aunt Mo backed out of the yard.

"So," Maureen said after a few minutes on the road. "What *did* happen between you and Corey?"

Mya pressed her head against the headrest and closed her eyes. "You don't want to know."

"I wouldn't have asked if I didn't want to know," her aunt returned.

Massaging her brow to ward off the headache that was threatening to attack her, Mya expelled a sigh and said, "He found out about the baby. About the miscarriage. You didn't tell him, did you?"

"Nope," was her aunt's response.

Mya looked over at her. "Is that all you have to say?"

"Am I supposed to say anything else?" Maureen asked. "I wasn't allowed to say anything fifteen years ago, back when you lost the baby. You begged me to keep quiet."

She twisted in the passenger seat to stare at her aunt. "Are you saying I should have told him then?"

"Of course you should have," Maureen said, as if they were talking about telling Corey that Mya had ruined his favorite shirt.

She threw both hands in the air. "You tell me this *now*? Fifteen years later? Why didn't you say it back then, Mo?"

Without warning, Maureen jerked the wheel to the side, sending the car careening onto the road's dusty shoulder. She cut the engine, then turned to Mya.

"You may not want to hear this, but you are Elizabeth's daughter through and through. You are as stubborn and as selfish as your mother. And just like her, you think making it out of Gauthier makes you better than everyone else."

"That's not true," Mya gasped, hurt and shock volleying against the walls of her chest at her aunt's unexpected attack.

"Oh, yes it is," Maureen insisted. "All you could ever talk about was getting out of this town. You were going to travel the world, then head to New York and become a big-name fashion designer. That didn't pan out the way you thought it would, did it? Maybe it wasn't this town that was holding you back, Mya. Maybe it was your small-mindedness."

Mya flinched as the words her aunt hurled at her hit like a bullwhip. She covered her face with her hands, the tears cascading down her cheeks like an uncontrollable waterfall.

"I thought you were proud of me," she choked out.

"I am proud of you," Maureen said. "But I wasn't proud of the way you left. Or how you stayed away all these years."

Her aunt captured her left wrist and tugged until Mya pulled her hand away from her face. She cupped her chin and gently urged Mya to look up.

"You know I have always loved you as if you were my own child. And I swear, Mya, you could get away with just about anything before I get angry with you." Maureen lifted her chin up a bit more and stared at her, understanding shining in her eyes. "But you owed it to Corey to tell him about the baby after you lost it."

"I was scared," Mya whispered.

"I know you were," Maureen said, finally

letting go of Mya's face. "Maybe I should have pushed you a little harder to tell him. It's bothered me all these years."

"I never should have come back here," Mya said.

"Dammit!" Maureen slammed her hands on the steering wheel. "Mya Eloise Dubois, how hardheaded can you be?"

"What?" Mya yelled.

"You never should have left," her aunt stated. "Not the way you did. And you shouldn't have stayed away this long. That's the point I'm trying to make. This is your home. The people here . . . *we* are your home. Stop running, Mya. You're better than that."

Mya swiped at the tears still flowing down her cheeks.

Her aunt was right. This town, these people, they embodied every notion of home she'd ever had. Despite how much she had grown to love New York, if she was being honest with herself, Mya could admit that something had always been missing. She had found that missing piece the minute she'd set foot in Gauthier again. She'd found it when Corey Anderson had approached her at her grandfather's funeral and reminded her of everything she'd given up when she'd run from Gauthier all those years ago.

She didn't want to run anymore. She wanted that sense of home forever. And she wanted it with Corey.

"Aunt Mo." Mya sniffed. "Can you turn around? I need you to bring me somewhere."

"Depends on where I'm bringing you," Maureen said, turning over the ignition.

Mya looked over at her. "I think you know."

Corey pushed the lawn mower across grass he'd already cut. Not that it mattered. He was trimming a lawn he hadn't been asked to trim. He'd hoped focusing on his neighbor's lawn would prevent him from gazing up at the sky and wondering if every airplane that flew overhead was the one bringing Mya back to New York. So far it wasn't working.

He'd had to stop himself from driving over to the Dubois house twice last night, then again this morning.

What in the hell was wrong with him? How could he even think about running to her after the lies she'd told, the secrets she'd held?

The woman had kept knowledge of their baby from him. They'd created a life together. The fact that the baby had not made it shouldn't have any bearing on the situation. He'd had a right to know.

Had it been a boy or a girl? He wondered if Mya even knew. Corey doubted he'd ever find out.

His palms clenched tightly around the lawn mower handle as an overwhelming fury tore through him. As quickly as it came, his anger started to abate. His rage was warranted, but what good would it do if he allowed it to consume him?

He'd expected Mya to forgive him for the mistakes he'd made back when they were teenagers. How much of a hypocrite would it make him if he could not forgive her? She had been a frightened seventeen-year-old girl who had just caught the father of the unborn child she lost having sex with another girl. How could he blame her for running and never looking back?

The last time she had left Gauthier she had stayed away for fifteen years. Who knew how long she would stay away this time? Just a few days ago, he had been preparing to take his and Mya's renewed courtship to the next level by asking her to move into his home. Now he was preparing for a life without her.

With an ache that settled like an anvil in

his gut, Corey accepted the very real possibility that he would never see her again. It carried with it a mind-numbing pain, one that would take everything he had within him to recover from.

Corey felt a tap on his shoulder. He let go of the lawn mower handle, turned and for a moment wondered if his pining for Mya was making him delusional. He looked past her and spotted Maureen's car idling in his driveway next door.

"Aunt Mo drove me here," she said unnecessarily. "We were on our way to the airport, but I couldn't do it, Corey." She shook her head, looking at the ground. When she looked up again, her eyes were soaked with unshed tears. "I couldn't leave here without apologizing."

Her voice cracked on the last word, and Corey had to force himself not to grab her and pull her into his arms.

"I was afraid. That's the only excuse I have. I was so, so afraid back then." She sniffed and wiped at her eyes. "I know it was wrong not to tell you about the baby, but after I left, I just didn't see the point. There was nothing anyone could have done about it."

"I could have been there for you, Mya."

She gave him a sad smile. "No, you

couldn't have. You were going off to college, and everyone knew you would make it to the major leagues. I didn't want the baby to keep you in Gauthier any more than I wanted it to keep me here." She shook her head. "None of that really matters anymore. I just . . . It was a mistake keeping it from you. You deserved to know. And I'm sorry, Corey. I am so sorry."

Despite the hurt she'd caused him, he loved her too much to hold it against her a second longer. He needed this woman in his life. Forever.

"Don't make another mistake, Mya." He reached for her, capturing her hand. "Don't leave."

"I have to," she said, and his heart sank. "My work is in New York. I love what I do, and I'm not giving it up." She paused. "But I don't want to give you up either."

Corey's chest tightened with cautious hope.

"I wondered if I could propose a compromise," she continued.

"I'm listening," Corey answered.

"I can divide my time between New York and Louisiana during the school year. In the summer, when school lets out, you come to New York. Is that something you would be willing to do?"

Corey pulled her to him, wrapping his arms around her and squeezing so tight he was afraid he'd break her. But he couldn't let go. He never wanted to let her go.

He pulled back slightly and looked into the face of the girl who'd stolen his heart all those years ago.

"There's nothing I wouldn't do for you, Peaches. I'd do anything. Everything. All you have to do is ask."

"I love you, Corey. I always have."

"I've never stopped loving you, Mya. You own my heart." He kissed her lips. "Can I do one thing?"

"What?" she said.

He gestured to his house next door. "Can I please take you home?"

She rested her head against his chest and tightened her arms around his waist.

"I'm already there."

ABOUT THE AUTHOR

Farrah Rochon had dreams of becoming a fashion designer as a teenager, until she discovered she would be expected to wear something other than jeans to work every day. Thankfully, the coffee shop where she writes does not have a dress code. When Farrah is not penning stories, the avid sports fan feeds her addiction to football by attending New Orleans Saints games.

The employees of Thorndike Press hope you have enjoyed this Large Print book. All our Thorndike, Wheeler, and Kennebec Large Print titles are designed for easy reading, and all our books are made to last. Other Thorndike Press Large Print books are available at your library, through selected bookstores, or directly from us.

For information about titles, please call:
  (800) 223-1244

or visit our Web site at:
  http://gale.cengage.com/thorndike

To share your comments, please write:
  Publisher
  Thorndike Press
  10 Water St., Suite 310
  Waterville, ME 04901